"Can you really be that naive?"

Wolfe asked her. "Or is it just an act?" There was derision in his voice. "Let's find out, shall we?"

Before Lindsey had a chance to guess his intentions, he caught her by the shoulders and pulled her close to him.

"No!" Her hands went up and she struck out at his chest, but his mouth came down to cover hers and she was lost.

Her mind was cool and clear, but the moment his lips touched hers, her body began to melt and nothing else mattered.

"So," his drawl was obvious as he finally released her. "Now we've proved that you have at least some of the responses of a normal adult female."

Lindsey stood there as he turned and left her. How dared Wolfe make love to her, and how could she have been such a fool as to respond?

He Was the Stranger

Sheila Strutt

Harlequin Books

TORONTO • NEW YORK • LONDON
AMSTERDAM • PARIS • SYDNEY • HAMBURG
STOCKHOLM • ATHENS • TOKYO • MILAN

Original hardcover edition published in 1985
by Mills & Boon Limited

ISBN 0-373-02754-0

Harlequin Romance first edition March 1986

CHAPTER ONE

HE had arrived. At least, the powerful-looking white car parked out front in the driveway of the house had most certainly not been there when she had ridden off. Lindsey Kinsale set the chestnut quarter horse at a fast gallop down the shallow slope of the swale behind the house, aware that her heart was beating shallowly and her breath was coming fast. If it was Wolfe Manston's car he had not just arrived, but he had done so far earlier than she had been told to expect him.

The ground levelled out and they went thudding past the marshy slough, dry now and empty with no red-winged blackbirds quarrelling on the stripped, bare reeds. Jake would disapprove if she brought Fire Bird back in a lather, but for once, Jake Heshka's disapproval was the least of her concerns. She should anyway have learned by now that it was pointless to expect, or even try for, Jake's approbation. Jake had been her uncle's man, and it was a man's world at Milk River.

The most amazing thing, once the house had blocked the white car from her view, was how everything still looked the same. The house with its weathered roof of silvery cedar shakes; the barns; the dug-outs where the cattle drank; everything, down to the last tree in the windbreak, looked just the same, and yet, with Ben Manston's death two months before, everything had begun to change.

And, if her guess about the ownership of the white car was correct, in the next few minutes her own life was about to undergo the greatest change of all.

'He's here!' More friend than housekeeper, Adeline Littlebear put an end to her speculation immediately Lindsey went through the kitchen door. 'He came about ten minutes after you went out. I put him in the office!' A face the colour of a nicely toasted bun with black currants for eyes shone with a mixture of excitement and conspiracy. The singsong voice, however, stayed low and guarded as if the man several doors and walls away could still hear every word.

'What's he like?' Lindsey glanced down at the sleeveless quilted vest she had on over a denim jacket and denim jeans which were worn and faded at the thighs and knees. Had she got time to change, or not? She had not, she decided, and settled for going across and rinsing her hands at the kitchen sink. What she looked like was hardly likely to be Wolfe Manston's first concern. It was Milk River he had come to see and—her heart clenched—take away.

'What's he like? Well, let me see!' Adeline raised her voice to compete with the sound of running water. 'He's tall—not specially so,' she qualified, 'but it's more than that! He's got this way of looking at you as if there's absolutely no doubt that you're going to do exactly what he wants!'

Lindsey stopped listening. For all her North American Indian ancestry, Adeline was no more prescient than anybody else when it came to reading minds. What affected her was what Wolfe Manston had decided she should do. Not that it really mattered. She had already made up her mind to leave. The ranch had been not just her home but her world ever since she had been orphaned by a car crash eighteen years earlier, but without Ben Manston there, it could never be the same again. The only thing she had not yet settled with herself was when she should make the break and, if he wished, Wolfe Manston had a perfect right to tell her to leave that night.

'He's already asked me if I'll stay on, and he was real nice about it!' Adeline supplied at least a hint of what might lie in the immediate future. 'Considerate! A real gentleman, in spite of everything!' Adeline had also been horrified that a total stranger could be summoned across the world to take everything. She handed Lindsey a towel from the rack. 'He ain't married, neither!' Her wishful thinking had all the subtlety of a passing train.

'I know that!' Lindsey snapped—and immediately regretted it. But it was tiresome. The man had been in the house less than an hour and Adeline was already seeing him as a potential husband!

If only it wasn't so isolated and out of the world's mainstream up here. If only being unmarried at twenty-five didn't make her the local curiosity in a society in which everyone, it seemed, had picked out their future spouses before they even left high school.

If only she could tell everyone about Derek—but Derek was adamant about that.

Besides which, Wolfe Manston was old enough to be her father—or her father's father's cousin, or whatever his relationship had been to Uncle Ben. It had taken two months to find him and, when found, he had been travelling in a remote part of the Australian outback. When the lawyer had called her to break the news, Lindsey had not paid too much attention when the intricacies of kinship were explained. He was a man, that was all that mattered, because, even in this day and age, only a man could inherit at Milk River.

'Where is he, Adeline?' Lindsey silenced the sound of distant wedding bells in Adeline's ears.

She looked reproachful. 'I told you! I put him in the office. He wanted to see the books, so I showed him through!'

'Then I guess I'd better go through, too, and get it over with!' Lindsey took off her quilted vest and denim jacket and checked that her blue plaid shirt was still tucked in neatly round her waist. She then put up a hand and smoothed back hair the colour of bleached wheat straw left in the fields in winter.

She wore it tied back with a ribbon when she was working—and she *was* still working. Otherwise, she had darker brows, almost purple eyes, and a chin that put her face on the determined side of oval—and they would have to do exactly as they were.

'That's right!' Adeline nevertheless was incorrigible. 'Make a good first impression, I always say. No harm ever came from that! I thought I might bring coffee through in about ten minutes.' Nothing was going to stop her seeing how things were getting on.

'Yes, do!' What use was there in fighting over already well fought ground?

Lindsey left the kitchen and walked along the

narrow passageway to the hall. Unwilling to leave
the whole house open with only the two of them
and Adeline living there, Ben Manston had closed
off most of it and the hall was used as a living room
with a log fire crackling in the hearth. The landing,
running round three sides at first-storey level, was
reached by a big, wide staircase, but the bedrooms
leading off that landing were never used. The three
of them slept in bedrooms at the top of a separate
flight of back stairs leading from the kitchen.

The farm office, so called from years of use, was
down a short corridor off to one side of the hall, and
when she reached it, Lindsey stood outside the
door, wondering if she should knock or not.

It seemed more like eternity than months since
she had shared that office with her uncle, and yet it
was still only three months since the condition had
been diagnosed that had turned Ben Manston from
a hale and hearty rancher in his mid-fifties, with
years of life ahead of him, to a dying man.

She tilted back her head to stop the tears and the
gesture gave her courage and a touch of pride. She
would not knock, because Milk River was still her
home, but it was hard to turn the knob and go
inside.

'Yes? What is it?' The figure sitting with his back
to her at what had always been Ben Manston's desk
sounded annoyed.

'I'm sorry!' She had no need to apologise; she
had a perfect right to come into the room! 'You
wanted to see me.'

'Did I?'

'Yes.' She looked at the bent dark head. 'I'm
Lindsey Kinsale.'

He swivelled round to face her and everything went dead.

This couldn't be! This just couldn't be! The Wolfe Manston she had been expecting was in his fifties—sixties!—not a finely honed man of thirty-eight or nine getting easily to his feet.

He was dark with a Spaniard's darkness and the air of a buccaneer. Not over-tall—for once Adeline had been right. He only had to incline his head to look down when he reached her—his impact came from the aura of force and will emanating from every line of the lean hard body in the well cut city suit.

He must sometimes see fit to laugh or smile, because a network of tiny lines fanned out from the corner of his slate grey eyes but, in repose, his face would always carry the look it carried now. A hardness that balanced purpose against sentiment with, when it came to a decision, sentiment taking second place.

The rest—the thinly bridged nose, the thick dark hair, the deep lines etched on either side of the finely shaped mouth—was almost automatically assimilated for recall later when she was alone, away from the sheer presence of the man.

'You say you're Lindsey Kinsale?' He was looking at her as if he doubted it.

'Yes!' Her hand had somehow been taken up in his and she removed it. 'Yes,' she said more firmly. 'Yes, I am.'

Was she also not what he had expected? She saw the shadow of what could have been surprise darkening the surface of those slate-grey eyes, and wondered. With a name like Lindsey, people sometimes expected her to be a boy, not a tall, slim—skinny was Lindsey's word—woman with small, high breasts and a neat, trim waist.

'In that case,' he said, 'you'd better come in and sit down.'

Wolfe Manston had been born in Quebec, the lawyer had told her. He had been born in French Canada, two thousand miles east of here. Wolfe Manston would also have a touch of French left in his voice—just an edge, like velvet, to soften the clipped sound. It ran along her spine and, hearing it, Lindsey could no longer be in any doubt. This really was Wolfe Manston.

He pulled the chair out from the desk she used, set at an angle to her uncle's, and motioned her into it.

She sat and watched him. He went back to her uncle's chair and tilted it on its swivel until the thin October sunshine was brilliant on her face, but his was difficult to read.

'We seem to be facing a difficult situation.'

Was there hostility in his look? If there was, it would hardly be surprising. If she had not existed, there would have been nothing to encumber his inheritance. Milk River and all it held would have been his, clear and free, without the complication of settling the future of a hitherto unknown and very distant relative. He might have made a wrong assumption about her sex, but he must have known that the ranch had been her home since she had been a child.

'Before we start discussing anything, however, I would like you to know that I'm sorry about your

uncle's death. I never met him, but I'm told he was
a fine man.'

His sympathy was totally unexpected. 'Yes, he
was.' Lindsey's voice shook. Seeing his successor
sitting there, a totally unfamiliar figure in the so
familiar chair, made her realise for the thousandth
time just how much she missed Ben Manston and
would do for years to come.

The eyes and ears missed nothing. 'Would you
prefer it if we talked somewhere else?'

'No.' She shook her head and swallowed hard.
'Where could we go? He's a part of every room!'
She tried a watery smile. 'It's just that sometimes—
sometimes, I can't believe that he won't just come
walking in.'

'I know what you mean.' Did he? Did he really
know how hard it sometimes was to accept that she
would never see that craggy face again? The rough,
almost raw edge to his voice told her that he might.
It struck a chord and she felt herself warm to him.
'So,' he broke the sudden silence unemotionally,
'what are your plans? It must have been a shock to
find out that a total stranger could inherit everything—or did you know?'

'I grew up knowing it.' Milk River was a man's
world and Milk River went to sons. Daughters were
married off and, like her own mother, went elsewhere. It was the eldest son who inherited, and it
had been that way since the first Wolfe Manston
had come to Canada and carved his empire from
the prairie bush. Four generations had gone since
then and no one had envisaged that, one day, there
might be no sons and that it would be a woman with
all the moral right to inherit.

And even if the first Wolfe Manston had antici-
pated such a thing, it would still have been the
same. He had had six sons; those sons had sons;
there would always be a man somewhere to continue the name and the tradition, even if that man
had had to come halfway across the world.

And the old patriarch had been right. The wheel
had come full circle and it was his namesake now
sitting watching her with shadows making a mystery of his thoughts.

'As far as my plans are concerned,' Lindsey
spread her fingers and looked down at them, 'I've
not made any yet.' Then, because she didn't want
his patronage—because she, too, was a descendant
of that first Wolfe, 'not that I'm not qualified to get
a job somewhere else!'

It came out in a rush, and Derek would be
furious. She had rights, Derek had insisted. It was
ridiculous in this day and age that she got nothing
from the estate, and one way to secure those rights
would be to stay exactly where she was in the hope
of forcing some sort of settlement. Not, she suspected, that this Wolfe Manston, any more than the
original, was likely to be amenable to either force
or pressure.

'There's no hurry.' The smile came back. 'I
wasn't planning on cutting you off without a dime
or throwing you out tonight!'

The smile made him look younger, and she suddenly had the strangest feeling that she had seen
him somewhere before. That was impossible, of
course. Although he had been born in Canada, his
father had been a civil engineer and he had spent
his whole life, from early childhood, travelling the

world. It had bred a wanderlust, and that was why,
the lawyer had explained, he had been so difficult
to locate.

'Anyway, take as long as you like to make up
your mind,' Wolfe said. 'Anything you regard as
your own personal property is, of course, still
yours. You've got a pony you care about, I
believe?'

'A horse.' Amusement at the idea of the highly
strung Fire Bird being regarded as a children's
mount touched Lindsey's high cheekbones with
colour and set highlights dancing in her purple
prairie crocus eyes. The potential of the woman
appeared briefly through the almost childlike face,
but all Lindsey saw was the head under its mane of
jet black hair snap sharply back and dark brows
draw together thoughtfully.

"One thing I am in a hurry about, though, is to
get this lot sorted out.' The subject of her future
had been dealt with and long brown fingers had
started to tap impatiently on the papers on the
desk. This was exactly how the first Wolfe must
have been; autocratic, single-minded, concerned
only with one thing; the future and survival of the
ranch.

"I've got an appointment with the lawyer tomorrow morning,' Wolfe went on talking through her
sudden insight, 'and I've been going through all
this. Who's been running the place for the past few
months?' he demanded suddenly. 'These,' he
tapped again, 'are a mess! Fine up until about a
month ago, maybe, but then they peter out. No
proper entries, just a few scribbled notes and a lot
of bills, most of them unpaid. God knows if the man

responsible was even honest, but he'll certainly have to be replaced.'

How could she, even for an instant, have warmed to him or thought he could have any sympathy? Anger worked its way up Lindsey's spine. How typical that he was already planning to make sweeping changes without even bothering to enquire about the cause, and how typical, how like a Manston, that he should automatically assume that anyone running a ranch of Milk River's scope and size must obviously be a man.

'I . . .' she started, but Wolfe swept her aside.

"I intend to run a business here, not a charity,' he stated flatly. 'And I mean to have it running at a profit, not, as I suspect it has been doing until now, limping along on the edge of loss because of general all-round inefficiency and misplaced sentiment!'

He paused for breath, and Lindsey seized her chance. 'If it interests you at all,' she bit out icily, '*I* was my uncle's ranch manager!'

His reaction was everything and more than she could have wanted. 'You?' He looked at her in total disbelief.

'Why not?' she retorted. 'They may not be important enough to be considered when it comes to an inheritance, but a lot of women are doing what was once considered to be men's work nowadays!'

And she was doing it because she had never wanted to leave the ranch. Her uncle had insisted. She was too innocent, too naïve—he hadn't used those words, but that was what he had meant—and when she left high school she must go somewhere else; see something of another world and have something to compare. So she had gone to univer-

sity and qualified in agriculture and management.
Her uncle had given in with good grace, and when
she had qualified and come back, he had let her
stay.

'So you're in charge here, are you?' Wolfe
studied her through half-closed eyes.

Lindsey flared up. 'I do have my degree, if that's
what bothers you!' she snapped belligerently.

'Really?' He seemed amused. 'Unfortunately,
all that proves is that you're qualified. What seems
to be in doubt,' he glanced down at the papers on
the desk, 'is your competence.'

'And you're not in the least interested in finding
out how things reached this state, I suppose!'
Goaded, Lindsey lashed back at him. She could
hardly recognise herself. 'Well, let me explain.
Since my uncle died—since,' she faltered and then
regained speed, 'he got sick, I've been doing all his
work on top of my own, and then, when we heard
that you'd been found, I lost my right to sign
cheques. That's why bills aren't paid and things
seem in a mess, but if you'll take the trouble to
check a little more, you'll see that nothing is fun-
damentally out of order and that a few hours' work
will put everything to rights.'

'So?' He regarded her angry face. 'Everything is
in good order, is it? In that case,' half-closed grey
eyes snapped open and he sat up straight, 'perhaps
you'll now be kind enough to explain this—and
this!'

He stabbed at pages with his finger, and for the
next few hours, Lindsey was kept busy supplying
detailed information to a keen and active brain that
had absorbed a great deal about High River in the

short time it had been focussed on the books. The coffee that Adeline brought in grew cold and was replaced by a working supper, eaten in the office from plates balanced on the desk. Lindsey scarcely noticed the time go by. She felt stimulated and inspired. For the first time since Ben Manston died, she really felt alive.

Eventually Wolfe pushed back his chair and stretched his legs. 'I think that's enough for today. I'm driving back to Saskatoon tonight and I'll be with the lawyer all day tomorrow. Meanwhile, as you indeed seem to be qualified,' he referred back to her earlier claim with his own very personal smile, 'I'd like you to carry on as manager. Think it over while I'm away and let me know.'

He swept out of the house with a minimum of leavetaking, treating the two-hundred-mile drive to Saskatoon as no more than a short trip down the road. And, watching the way he gunned the powerful sports car away along the drive, Lindsey had no doubt that he would push the speed limit all the way.

She shivered in the early evening cold and turned back into the house, aware of a sense of let-down and anti-climax. Adeline shut the door behind them both. Adeline, she knew, was disappointed that Wolfe was not going to stay, and as for her, her own reactions were too confused to draw any real conclusion.

Yesterday she had thought she might be going to have to leave. Now, Wolfe had offered her the chance to stay. It was the man himself who made the prospect daunting.

True, she had a grudging respect for him. His

ideas for the future of Milk River were good. He was right in thinking that a ranch which comprised not only itself but four subsidiary properties and a number of abandoned farmhouses now renovated and let out, should be making more of a profit than they had been doing in the last years of Ben Manston's life.

In fact, she hadn't realised how much her uncle had let things drift until his heir had brought his fresh eye to bear and everyone could benefit from some of his ideas.

It was the man himself; her mind kept on going back to that one same point. Memory assembled fragments of the whole and produced a lean, hard face, full of angles and straight lines and dominated by a pair of, at times, unbearably steady eyes.

Adeline's description also came back to her. 'A man who looks at you as if there's absolutely no doubt you're going to do exactly what he wants!' Lindsey felt the beginnings of an odd uneasiness, a stirring that made her vividly remember the cool, firm touch of his hand on hers.

But it was the weather! She had noticed when she came inside that there was going to be a storm, and the onset of the first storm of winter was always unsettling. In any event, as far as Wolfe's offer was concerned, she had no need to decide that night. Tomorrow—rain, hail or snow—she would be seeing Derek, and Derek would tell her exactly what she should do.

CHAPTER TWO

'HE couldn't have asked you to do anything that suited us better if he'd tried!' Obvious satisfaction filled Derek Foster's handsome, slightly fleshy, face.

Lindsey shook her head. 'But I thought it would be the last thing you'd want!'

'You know, Lin,' Derek was impatient, 'for a bright girl, you can sometimes be very dense! Of course it suits us!'

'Well, I'm afraid I don't understand.' Lindsey turned away and gazed out through the window of the farmhouse Derek rented.

The threatened storm had held off and she had ridden over there first thing that morning. Fire Bird was rugged up cosily outside, but in spite of the fire that smouldered in the iron stove in one corner, the atmosphere in the kitchen was far from cosy.

Her misgivings about staying on and working for Wolfe Manston had grown during the night. It was quite impossible, she had eventually decided. It was no longer the man himself who stopped her; she could deal with that. She had no need to go on wondering what was going on beneath the surface of those slate greys eyes each time they looked at her, and when enough time had passed, she would be used to him and he would not be such a fixture in her head. What she would never be used to, though, would be seeing him in Ben Manston's place. In his chair, his house, driving and riding across an open landscape that would for ever be associated with a far different face. A face that had been older, tireder, holding none of the clinical dispassion with which Wolfe had looked at things and decided there must be sweeping changes.

That was why she could never stay on and work for Wolfe Manston. It had nothing to do with the man himself, and that was what she had tried to explain to Derek and what Derek had refused to understand.

'We've been looking for a way to get you something out of the will, and this is it!' he said on a note of triumph. 'Now that Manston's asked you to stay on, he's showing he can't run the place without you, and no court in the country is going to throw out a case like that. We can challenge the will and win!'

Lindsey wished he would stop talking about the will. When they had first met, Derek was always saying that a struggling writer like himself had no need of money. Money was death to talent, he had proclaimed. He was even pleased when she had told him about the entailment on the ranch. If she had been able to inherit, they would have been tied down. This way, he said, they could go anywhere—anywhere in the world. The only thing that mattered was that they should be together.

It was only when the will was read that he had been appalled. Lindsey had always known, but Derek could not believe that everything—stocks, shares, bonds, everything—went with the ranch to Wolfe. All Lindsey was entitled to was her savings from the sizeable salary her uncle had insisted on paying her, and Annabel, the ancient car that he had given her eight years before when she had surprised everyone by passing the driving test at her first attempt.

Derek had clutched at the fact that the will had been drawn up before Lindsey had arrived as a sorrowful eight-year-old in Ben Manston's life.

'It's so unfair!' he kept repeating bitterly. 'If he'd known what was going to happen, he would have made another will. It's not all entailed, you could have had some of it. You've got to fight and prove your claim. If you don't want to do it for yourself, do it for him!' Then, seeing he had gone too far, he would come up to her and take her gently in his arms. 'I'm not interested in the money,' he would whisper, 'you know that. I just want my girl to get what should be hers.'

He did it now, turning her gently round from the farmhouse window, a lock of curly blond hair falling across his forehead and a look of little-boy contrition filling his blue eyes. 'I don't give a damn about the money,' he murmured softly, 'I just want my girl to have her rights!'

Lindsey relaxed against him, comforted by his body warmth. Of course he was only thinking of her. This was the man she knew and loved; romantic and full of artistic temperament; the man who had blazed into her life with all the brilliance of a comet when she had been in the corner store one day and he had come in, looking for a place to rent.

That had been four months ago; before Ben Manston's swift, final illness had been diagnosed, before the numbing shock of its discovery had driven everything else from her mind, but, in those few weeks of ecstatic happiness, she had at last discovered what it was to be in love.

She could still hardly believe that someone as handsome and talented as Derek had ever noticed her, far less have wanted to ask her out. She was so ordinary and unremarkable—fortunate to have an uncle like Ben Manston to take her in and give her so much love when her parents had been killed, but otherwise, completely ordinary and unremarkable in every way.

'You've got to stay!' Derek was persuasive. 'Now that Manston's asked you, stay and work for him. It needn't be for long—just long enough to prove how indispensable you are, and then we'll go to court and sue for half of everything he's got!'

'If you're sure?' Lindsey looked up doubtfully.

'Of course I'm sure.' Derek took his hands from around her waist and impatiently ran one through his long fair hair. 'Heaven knows I'd like nothing better than to be able to take you away from here, but that wouldn't be fair—to you,' he added hastily. 'I want my girl to have the best of everything, and I can't give you that.'

'But one day you will!' Lindsey reminded him.

'What?' Derek looked fractionally puzzled, but then his face relaxed. 'Oh, yes—the book, you mean. Of course when that gets published and on the best-seller lists, I'll be able to give you everything, but I can't even begin to think about writing while all this is going on.'

'I know.' Lindsey looked up into his intense face. It was her fault he couldn't concentrate on his writing, and it was unfair of her to be disappointed that he had not suggested they announce their secret engagement and get married straight away as a solution to the predicament Wolfe had created. On the ride across from Milk River, she had half expected that he would.

'Then you'll do it?' Derek was once more all eagerness. 'You'll stay on and work for him? You won't be able to break the entailment on the property, but if you can prove how much you've contributed, you should at least get some of the cash.'

As Lindsey hesitated, his lips set in a stubborn line, giving him the look of a small boy who feels he has been cheated and is looking for a way to pay back. It was a look she hated and she would do anything to chase it away. She flung her arms around his neck.

'All right,' she said, 'I'll stay!'

With her arms linked round his neck, Derek picked her up and swung her round, the sheer, uncomplicated satisfaction on his face more than her reward. He held her to him for a moment and then set her gently on her feet. 'If only you knew how much I hate my girl having to do this,' he said huskily. 'Knowing that you'll be up there with him all the time when I want you here with me!'

The pressure of his hands and body grew more urgent and he buried his face in the angle of her neck.

'No, Derek, please!' Lindsey began to tense.

'No,' he said, 'you're right.' She had done no more than begin to stiffen before he put her from him, gently and yet with an air of restrained passion burning in his face. 'I want you more than I can say,' he told her hoarsely, 'but no—you're right. We'll wait.'

Five minutes later, riding back across the fields, Lindsey could still hear the fervour in Derek's voice and taste and feel the pressure of his lips.

Some men would have pressured her—she might not be worldly, but she was not totally naïve—but Derek respected not exactly a reluctance but more of a reserve that made her draw a strict line which she could not cross.

But then Derek was so special. Who else would have even taken a second look at her that day when he came into the store? The only pressure he had put on her had been to do something about how she looked.

'You make me feel embarrassed!' he had teased her. 'You look about fifteen. People will think I'm cradle-snatching!'

So they had driven into Saskatoon, and Derek had almost supervised while the stylist had cut her fine blonde hair from waist to shoulder length, and most of the dress clothes in her wardrobe now had been Derek's choice.

Even her uncle had approved of that particular influence. 'You're getting to look more like your mother every day,' he had said one day shortly before he died. 'She was a lovely girl.' He relapsed back into silence on his pillows and Lindsey had blinked the tears back from her lashes.

Dear Derek! How she loved him—and he her. If it was hard for her to go back to Milk River and face the next few months, how much harder must it be for him to let her go.

And as for failing to understand exactly how she

felt about staying on with a stranger in her uncle's house, how could he be expected to understand? Derek had never had a proper home. His rich, divorced parents had pushed him on one side so that they could be free to lead their own lives without the encumbrance of an unwanted child.

Home for Derek had been a series of expensive boarding school, some of them in Europe, then university and then acting and stage design before the small annuity had come along that had freed him of the need to make a living and let him seek the solitude of the prairies to fulfil the creative urge he had to write.

How lucky she was that he had chosen this particular area, and how more than lucky that he had chosen her.

She crested a slight slope above the white, alkaline-edged river that gave the ranch and the little town nearby its name, and Milk River with its house and outbuildings lay beneath her like a toy.

The first Wolfe had started in a sod house and there had been oxen and ox carts in the barns, not today's prize-winning cattle and expensive agricultural machinery. After the sod house had come a frame house—it was still there; used as a barn for Adeline's chickens—but when old Wolfe and his sons had begun to prosper, they had started buying up more land and the house they built then had had to be bigger, grander, more impressive than anything ever dreamed of by the neighbours they had bought—or manoeuvred—out.

She could see it now; an immigrant's dream of a Colonial mansion, all wings and roofs and pillared porticos. The symbol of the empire the first Wolfe had built, and as out of place in so much emptiness as a cuckoo in a sparrow's nest.

The thought of the first Wolfe brought another face to mind; dark, assessing, summing up, with a rare slow smile like warmth on a cold night. Lindsey pushed Fire Bird into a loping trot. Wolfe, this Wolfe, was coming back in about eight hours' time. She had work to do, and however many misgivings she might still have about staying on, she was good at what she did and she planned to prove it.

'We might as well go on up, then.' Adeline stacked the last dish and looked at her across the kitchen.

'Yes, I guess we might.' Lindsey had never felt more of a fool. Working all day—that was acceptable. Working until both her head and eyes ached from the effort of clearing her own desk as well as Ben's. When she had finished, there was nothing with which any man could possibly find fault, but if she just thought of Wolfe as 'any man', why had she then rushed to shower and change, keeping one eye on the clock and shedding jeans and shirt in favour of a dress and brushing her pale hair until it curved smoothly in between her shoulders and her chin?

Adeline knew, but then Adeline had also gone to extra trouble, producing a roast in the middle of the week, when there were just the two of them to eat it. Because Wolfe had not come back.

For some peculiar reason, Lindsey realised, she was building him up to immense proportions in her mind. Even when she went to bed, she found herself listening for the sound of his car arriving in the yard. It was only vaguely, half asleep, that she thought she heard it, and when she went to her window the next morning and looked out, she would not have been surprised to find the yard quite empty. But the car was there; no longer white and shiny but dirty and streaked with mud with every sign of having been driven hard.

She checked her watch. Not quite seven. If Wolfe had not come back until the small hours, he must still be asleep. She checked his door as she went past; two along from hers with Adeline's room and a bathroom in between. Uncle Ben's old room. There was no sign of sound or movement, so he *must* still be asleep. Reassured, Lindsey went down the front stairs leading to the hall, then through the swing door and on towards the kitchen.

This time, she would be prepared. This time, when she saw him, she would not be taken by surprise. There would be no shock. When he eventually came down to breakfast, she would be sitting there, waiting, prepared to see him. A perfectly ordinary man, not a tyrant or an ogre, just a man whom fate had given an unfair amount of power over her own future. Put in those terms, the slight fluttering in her stomach seemed ridiculous.

The kitchen door was partly open. She pushed it and went in. Adeline was smiling—that was her first reaction. Adeline never smiled; she snorted sometimes and her black eyes twinkled, but Adeline *never* smiled. Her second reaction was that Wolfe was there.

He was also smiling, leaning back in his chair with grey eyes glinting, and something inside Lindsey clenched.

Cream cords had taken the place of the formal

suit he had been wearing the first time she had seen
him. Cream cords and an unbleached woollen
sweater over an open-necked shirt that threw the
dark skin of his face and throat into sharp relief.
Seeing him so relaxed and unaware, a twinge of an
older memory once more flashed across her mind,
but it must be because something about him reminded her of Uncle Ben. It wasn't obvious—Ben
Manston had never had the razor edge of that face
and jaw—but there must be something. Perhaps it
was the ease and the authority with which his
successor filled her uncle's high-backed chair, but,
whatever the cause of the uneasy feeling of *déjà-vu*,
the Wolfe Manston of the here and now was everything and more than she remembered and he
frightened her.

'Good morning.' For an instant his smile
included her.

'Good morning.' She stood there woodenly and
watched it die. What did she say now? That she
hadn't expected to see him down so early? That she
had somehow expected him to be different? If that
had been her hope, it was mistaken. The mouth and
chin were just as firm, the eyes as level, the feeling
that they could see right through her was just as
strong. And Derek wanted her to say and get the
upper hand!

Derek. Of course, she had Derek. Lindsey
started to relax. 'I didn't think you'd be up so soon.'
She was pleased with her degree of casualness.

'Why not?' He sounded just as casual. 'I've no
intention of letting a blow-out dominate my life.'

So that was what had happened; why he had not
come back the previous evening. A puncture, a

burst tyre somewhere on the highway between here and Saskatoon. Of all the many reasons she had thought of, she had missed one of the most obvious.

'You want breakfast?' Adeline stopped the crazily swinging pendulum of her reaction.

'No, thanks—just coffee.'

'I think you'd better eat.'

'Oh? Why?' Lindsey paused on her way to her chair.

'You'll need it. I want you to show me round.'

'The ranch?'

'Unless you can think of a better place to go.' He was mocking her, and Adeline was on his side.

'I thought you'd want to go over the books again.' Lindsey remembered the hours she'd spent the previous day putting them to rights.

'I've seen the books. Now I want to see the real thing—for myself!' he added ominously. 'From some of the things the lawyer had to say, I think it's about time an outsider had a look at what's happening here.'

Lindsey's chin went up. 'Are you accusing me of dishonesty, or just incompetence?'

'Neither.' His look speared through her in two dark shafts of grey. 'Unless you think I would be justified?'

Even Adeline was shocked. 'Here,' she put a plate of pancake and sausage in front of Lindsey, 'I'll go tell Jake to gas up the truck.'

'I'll go.' Lindsey was halfway to her feet.

'No—stay here. I want to talk to you.'

Lindsey sat. No one—no one—ever talked to her like that. People might gossip about her behind her back, but being Ben Manston's niece had made her one apart. She had acquaintances but no friends. No boy-friends, even at university—until, that was, Derek had blazed into her life.

Derek. The glow withstood the blast of cold air Adeline let in as she went out, only to die as Wolfe refocussed his attention back on her.

'I made you an offer before I left.' He was leaning back, long fingers idly crumbling a piece of bread, but there was nothing idle about the way he was watching her. 'Have you decided what you're going to do?'

'Yes.' She began to eat, refusing to look at him.

'So?' he prompted.

She took a breath. Of course she wasn't going to stay. She was going to leave, today, as soon as she could pack her things. She would have to explain to Derek, but Derek would understand. 'I'll stay.'

'Good.' His apparent satisfaction was as incomprehensible as her reply. When she had opened her mouth, it had been to give him a flat no. What awful gear-shift in her brain had made those two words come out? She opened her mouth again, but Wolfe was going on. 'In that case, we'll discuss salary and conditions of employment later. You'll carry on living in the house, of course,' he added, as if there could be no question, 'but as far as any sort of contract is concerned, shall we say a trial period of six months on either side?'

A different sort of stupefaction filled her. If she were to stay—*if*—it was for her own purposes, not his. She would be staying to prove that although she might be a woman in a man's world, she had rights—entitlements. The money involved in the will was secondary. It was, as Derek had so often said, a matter of principle. And now here she was, listening to Wolfe calmly laying down terms and conditions as if she had been begging to keep her job.

'I really don't think . . .'

His head went back as she began and his lips moved underneath half-closed eyes. 'If you thought I was employing you out of any misplaced feeling of sentiment or guilt, then you're quite wrong,' he drawled. 'I've asked you to stay firstly,' he emphasised, 'because nothing I've seen or heard so far indicates that you're not competent to run the ranch . . .'

'Thank you!' Her sarcasm was wasted.

'. . . and secondly, because I expect to be away a lot and I want some continuity.'

Lindsey absorbed the fact. If he was going to be away a lot, then perhaps the situation would be tolerable.

'However, as I don't insult competent people by doing them favours like a child, I want to make it clear that, while you do work here, it will be under the usual conditions that apply to any new employee and that—' he paused, '—usually means a trial period.'

He couldn't have made her status in his life more obvious. 'I hardly thought of myself as an employee when my uncle was alive,' she said defensively.

'No,' he agreed, 'I don't suppose you did. But looking back won't alter things. And as that sounds like Jake bringing the truck round,' he glanced towards the window: discussion closed, 'I suggest you go and change into something a little more suitable.'

Even if she had been going to leave, she would die first now! She was not only going to stay, she was going to get the best of him. When she had done that, *then* she would leave, but only on her terms.

Minutes later, upstairs in her room, Lindsey was still hot in the face as she struggled out of the skirt and blouse she had put on in anticipation of a day's work in the office and pulled on the cords and sweater that were much more suitable for scrambling in and out of the high seat of the half ton truck.

She could hear the engine running in the yard below her window and she could hear Wolfe's voice and Jake's. At least one person sounded happy— Jake. And four more people were going to be happy before the day was out. The tenants in the four subsidiary ranches High River also owned, to say nothing of their wives and daughters when they saw what an attractive man the new man was.

Damn! As she rummaged through her wardrobe looking for her heavy jacket, her hand caught a bunch of empty hangers and they fell clattering to the floor. She stooped to pick them up. Even now, she couldn't stop thinking what an attractive man Wolfe was. He had a completeness about him—an entirety. A quality that Uncle Ben had also had, but Derek somehow lacked.

'Damn!' This time she said it aloud. He was even making her disloyal to Derek. It was just that they looked different, that was all. Dark hair just had more impact than Derek's blond.

And she should know. She zipped her jacket and

pushed her pale locks firmly back. Before Derek, who had looked twice at her in her life?

Two men looked at her when she went out into the yard. A girl in blue cords and a matching fleece-lined bomber jacket and her cheeks touched with the flush of guilty indignation beneath purple sunset eyes.

Two men looked at her, but for a second, Lindsey saw only one.

'I've gassed her up, boss. Tank'll last you all day.' Jake's eyes went back to Wolfe, then to the gas pump in the corner of the yard, the truck and back again. Lindsey did not exist—and nor did Ben. There was a new boss at Milk River—a new man. For an instant she felt sick and lonely and totally left out.

'Here!' She hardly noticed Wolfe's hand on her elbow or saw him opening the red door of the truck.

What was it about this man that made everyone take to him so readily? First Adeline and now Jake. The pressure on her elbow ceased, and she sat in the high passenger seat and watched through the windshield as Wolfe walked round in front followed by a gesturing Jake. She hadn't known the usually surly and taciturn Jake could be so animated and alive; yellow teeth showing in a smiling mouth as he hung on every word. Even Toller, her uncle's old black labrador, had come out from the barn in which he lived and was making an effort to hoist himself after Wolfe when Wolfe finally got behind the wheel and gently shut the door in the moistly imploring face.

Lindsey shifted along the seat until her thigh almost touched the door. Whatever reactions she might have, she could push them on one side, and she did so as he put the automatic into gear. As far as she was going to be concerned, this was just another working day.

'Right! Pinder first, then Heshka—' Heshka was a common name hereabouts. Jake, still standing in the yard looking after them, might or might not be related to the tenant Wolfe was mentioning as they turned out of the gate into the drive, '—Hunt and the Jarulsowskis.'

He had done his homework well, Lindsey acknowledged grudgingly. He knew before she could tell him the order in which they should plan their day. One section of land comprised six hundred and forty acres, and six hundred and forty acres covered one linear mile. Milk River itself had twenty sections, bisected by the white alkaline-edged river that made everything possible. The others were five and ten sections each, give or take an acre, but to see them all in one day meant driving in the right direction, or else the prairie which stretched to infinity in all points of the compass would swallow them if they drove aimlessly.

All she had to do was point out grid roads and directions and sit there silently in four farm kitchens, as Wolfe absorbed the varying personalities of his tenants and they his.

'Are you hungry?' She could still see the Jarulsowskis when he asked the question. Standing in the yard; Hettie with a stunned expression on her face and Max still smiling broadly as their reflection receded in the truck's wing mirror.

'No, not really!' She was awash with coffee, and something else. The feeling that, as she had sat in each of the four kitchens and sipped as Wolfe and his new tenants talked, she—who had been in each of those four kitchens so many times before—was the outsider. And she resented it.

He was the stranger, and yet, sitting there, he could have been a part of Milk River all his life.

'Well, I am.' He referred back to his question, his profile clear and vital against the passing background of the stripped and stunted poplar bush. Lindsey felt something stir and savagely repressed it. She was sitting in this truck with her carefully maintained gap of three clear feet of leather seat between them for just one reason. To prove that she had rights. To prove, as Derek was insisting, that just because she was a woman, her claim against Milk River should not be overlooked.

'What?' She spoke aggressively and saw the face beside her set in its usual hard straight lines.

'Where do you suggest we go for lunch?'

'There's nowhere, really.' She wanted to go home, get away from him; have space to move outside the narrow confines of the truck.

'Isn't there?' He glanced at her. 'Didn't we go through a town earlier, and doesn't it have a hotel?'

'Yes, but—' She stopped. She could think of no convincing reason, but she didn't want to be alone with him. Talking, relaxing over a meal, it would be too easy to get caught up in the aura of general admiration that surrounded him. She didn't want to like him. She didn't want to be affected by his charm or his machismo, or whatever the fashionable word was nowadays for the indefinable something he obviously possessed.

She just wanted to get through the next six months, do her job and leave—with Derek.

'But what?' He glanced the question at her.

'Nothing.' Lindsey looked pointedly away at the flat landscape. 'If you really want to eat at the hotel, we turn down here and it's about five miles further on.'

A few heads turned, but their owners were looking at Lindsey as they went into the hotel. She was known—some of these people had been through high school with her. What she was not known for, however, was going out to lunch with an attractive man—with any man! Derek was insistent that they should never be seen together, but this particular newsflash would be all round the district in thirty minutes. If, that was, Hettie Jarulsowski hadn't already started the wires of the bush telegraph humming with her impressions of the man whom birth and blood had given such power over all their lives.

'The dining room's through here.' She led Wolfe past the curious glances and through the alcove leading from the lobby with a rigid back.

'Hi, Lindsey!' There was little trace of the Homecoming Queen of ten years earlier in the faded, middle-aged figure of the waitress coming up to them. That was what a work-shy husband and three children under five could do to you, Lindsey told herself vindictively. 'We don't often see you here!'

'No.' It was a man's world at Milk River, Lindsey warned herself—remember that.

'You eating?' Charlene Savitz fastened her eyes on Wolfe and a glimpse of the Homecoming Queen appeared behind the tired face.

'Yes—please.' She was behaving badly, she knew she was. Charlene was waiting for her to introduce them, but why should she? Everyone would know exactly who Wolfe was soon enough, even though the hotel was one of the few places that hadn't come to him with his inheritance.

'Is there a telephone I can use?' Wolfe paused in the act of stripping off his coat, dark and striking against the sheepskin lining.

'Yes, sure.' Charlene smiled back eagerly. 'It's through there in the lobby—I'll show you where.'

'I think I can manage.' He was alien, an outsider, even his voice was different from theirs, slightly husky and low-pitched with its French overtones. That in itself should have been enough to get him regarded with suspicion in this close-knit, almost insular community. Instead, he was regarded like the Second Coming.

Raucous laughter reached them from the adjoining beer hall. There was movement; chairs were scraping back. A party was breaking up, and Wolfe looked down at her. 'Are you going to be all right here on your own for a few minutes?'

'Of course.' Lindsey pulled the menu to her and presented him with the top of her smooth head. 'Why shouldn't I be?'

'Why not, indeed?' She could feel his look pass over her, mocking and amused, then she heard him turn and stride out of the room, leaving her chagrined and furious with herself.

Of course she would be all right. Who would even give her a second glance? She was behaving like a schoolgirl, spoiled and silly. She was behaving as if she was jealous.

'You'd better have the steaks.'

'What?'

Charlene was still lingering, torn between watching Wolfe and work.

'They're the only thing worth eating. Shall I order his blue rare?'

'Yes, I guess so.' And hers medium. Straight down the middle of the line. Part of the vast majority; ordinary, unremarkable Lindsey Kinsale.

Damn! With Charlene gone, Lindsey pushed her thoughts to something else—like who Wolfe had to call, for instance. He didn't know anyone. It must be her uncle's lawyer, she decided, in Saskatoon.

They were there before she noticed. Two young men, strangers, with faces flushed and voices slurred from too much lunchtime beer.

'Okay if we sit here?' The taller of the two at least made some attempt, but he stumbled as he pulled back the chair facing her. The second just sat down; collapsed, Lindsey thought, would be a more appropriate word.

'No, it's not.' They couldn't know who she was. The dining room was absolutely empty and no one, not even people with whom she had been to school, would come up and force their company on her. She was Ben Manston's niece—that was enough to keep her set slightly apart—but these two men were strangers; miners, maybe, on their way up north. To them, neither Ben Manston nor his niece meant anything.

'Aw, come on!' It was meant to be persuasive. 'You look as if you need a little company!'

Lindsey glanced round. Not only was the dining room quite empty, but her two uninvited companions were sitting between her and the door.

'I'd rather . . .' she began.

'I'm sure you would!' The drunker of the two men sniggered. 'But later, honey, later. I've gotta have something to eat first!'

To them it was excruciatingly funny, and they both laughed.

Lindsey didn't know why she was so panicked. It was lunchtime, the middle of the day. Charlene would be coming back soon and so would Wolfe. In fact, Wolfe was already coming through the doorway from the lobby.

He came on as if he hadn't noticed. Surely he should do something? He must see how drunk the two men were, leaning back and laughing with an off-key edge that could easily turn to violence, but he just came walking on as if no threat existed and pulled out the sole remaining empty chair.

'I'm sitting here, then, am I?' He sat, and the two melted away.

One moment they had both been lounging there, owning the world, or at least that part of it that had attracted their attention. The next, they were standing, struggling to be sober, with one of them even offering an apology.

'I'm sorry, man. We didn't realise what the score was!'

'Really?' Wolfe's voice even froze her. 'Then we'll take it as a genuine misunderstanding, shall we?'

'Yeah, sure!' The owner of the apologetic countenance started backing. 'No offence meant, ma'am. Have a nice day!' He was still apologising, still trying to retrieve the situation, while his friend was pulling him backwards towards the lobby.

Wolfe picked up the menu.

'I've already ordered.' Lindsey found her voice.

'Good.' Grey eyes no less cold and no less threatening studied her. 'You seem to have quite an effect on people!'

'Only when they don't know me.' Lindsey felt acutely uncomfortable.

"Really?' One black eyebrow rose. He knew her. He shouldn't do, but in that moment, he knew her right down to her most secret thoughts. 'Perhaps you underestimate yourself,' he said.

CHAPTER THREE

SHE had gone a whole afternoon without thinking about Derek once.

Lindsey realised only when, about a mile from home, Wolfe suddenly stopped the truck and she followed the direction of his eyes towards the farmhouse Derek rented.

'What's that?' Wolfe sounded more than idly curious, and Lindsey cursed herself.

It had been Milk River's turn that afternoon—a detailed inspection of the ranch that gave the whole area its name. Hours of seeing everything from a new perspective, of answering questions that had taxed her brain and left her head spinning.

Nothing had escaped Wolfe. Not the condition of the purebred Herefords or the amount of arable acreage that had been left to winter fallow with fall now drawing to a close. Even the wild mallards had attracted his attention, and a whistling, calling skein of Canada geese flying overhead in a ragged V-formation, late on their way south.

Wolfe had done the driving, and she had let him, sitting back when they had finished and accepting without question that he seemed to know the way. It was, after all, quite simple: the house was to the west and he was merely following the blood-red ball of the setting sun.

But she should have paid attention. She should not have sat back, reliving those few seconds in which the sweep of slate-grey eyes had seemed to expose her deepest secrets. She should have made sure that they came back round the north side of the final section, well away from Derek's farmhouse and the final secret Wolfe mustn't—couldn't—guess.

'It's a farmhouse.' She stated the obvious and caught his obviously impatient look. 'We—' this time she caught herself, '—you own it. It used to belong to a family called Kersey. They home-steaded it, but the first Wolfe bought them out.' After they had broken up the land and started something that he wanted, the first Wolfe—and his sons—had either bought, or forced, the Kerseys out. 'We rent it out. Not the land,' she added quickly, 'we farm that. Just the house.'

'Oh? Who to?' Wolfe kept the back of his head towards her.

'A writer.' She avoided Derek's name.

'Really?' There was interest in his voice as he turned back from his inspection of the tiny, two-roomed wooden farmhouse. 'What does he write?'

'Well, nothing yet.' Lindsey saw his expression change and lose interest. 'But he will,' she went on hotly, 'just as soon as he's had time to settle in. He hasn't been there long—only a few months. He's just waiting for the right moment to get started.'

She wondered about the sudden urge that made her champion him so fiercely. Derek hardly needed anyone to defend him. She knew how talented he was.

A look she couldn't pinpoint crossed the space

between them. 'You seem to know him well,' he observed.

'Yes—quite.' It was hot in the truck—suddenly quite unbearably hot. Lindsey felt herself begin to flush. 'Do you want to go and meet him?' Nervous bravado made her ask the question.

'No, not today.' Wolfe put the truck in gear. 'I don't like the way he throws his rubbish out at the back, but apart from that . . . provided he pays his rent, I'll let him be.'

Rent! Lindsey looked studiously straight ahead through the windshield. Derek's rent had been one of the things that had been allowed to slip ever since Ben Manston's illness had first been diagnosed.

Her uncle had been oddly reluctant to let Derek rent the house, and Lindsey knew that if he had been well enough to notice, the arrears would never have been allowed to mount up the way they had.

As it was, Derek had already been four weeks behind when her uncle died, but, as he had never mentioned it, Lindsey had not liked to bring the subject up.

It was fortunate that the matter of Derek's unpaid rent had not caught the attention of the silent man behind the wheel beside her when he had been closeted with the books. Small though the amount was when compared with the overall turnover of the estate, it was still significant. Lindsey thanked whichever god had been watching over her. A reason for Derek's unpaid rent was not something she would have wished to give.

They were almost home when Wolfe suddenly stopped the truck again. Milk River was ahead of them in the half light, touched with pearl from the sunset and curiously impressive.

'It's humbling, isn't it?' There was a catch in Wolfe's quiet voice. 'Generations have lived and worked and loved and died to bring me here. I never even knew it existed, but now it's mine and I'm responsible. It's my responsibility to see that it continues—better than it was, not worse. I'm— what? A guardian for generations still to come?' He looked at her as if surprised to find her there. 'You must feel that, too?'

'Yes.' She did. It had been something of this sense of continuity, of guardianship, that had made it easy for her to accept that Milk River should continue in the Manston name. That, and a sense of kinship with that first Manston who had come out West into empty bush and made a world.

What was happening? Lindsey drew her shoulders back and sat up straight. In a minute, if she went on like this, she would start to like him. She, too, would fall under the powerful spell that had captivated Hettie Jarulsowski and all the rest.

'Home.' He said it quietly. 'At last—' she thought he said.

'I supposed you already had a home,' she said abruptly.

'I've had a lot, in most places in the world. You name it and I've probably lived there at some time. A travel writer covers a lot of territory.' He was back to his usual slightly mocking self, but this time Lindsey scarcely noticed.

A picture had flashed into her mind; grainy, black and white, it was of the head and shoulders of

a man talking about his work on the much abused
television set in the student common-room at university. Marc LeBrun, that was the name. No—
Marc LeBret, a travel writer; a rare bird in Canada,
particularly when his work was internationally
known.

But then Wolfe was rare, she realised, casting
him a sideways glance. No other man she had ever
met had had quite that air of self-possessed magnet-
ism. She could imagine him travelling on his own,
seeing the world from the unique perspective
that not only made his books one of a kind but
put his name almost constantly in the best-seller
lists.

'Why didn't you tell me?' The coincidence was
fantastic—two writers, Wolfe and Derek, living
within a mile of each other in this empty place.

'About *my* secret life?' Had Wolfe emphasised
the pronoun or had it been her imagination? Of
course it had, Lindsey decided. How could he know
about her and Derek and the plans they had? 'Why
should I tell you?' In the semi-darkness of fast
fading evening, the grey eyes gleamed. 'It was
rather refreshing not to have it known, for once. In
fact, I might just get to like being known as plain
Wolfe Manston!'

Plain? No, never plain. Complex, unusual, hard
to understand, but never plain.

'But John knows?' she queried.

'John?' For once, Wolfe looked puzzled.

'The lawyer.' And, Lindsey had thought, her
friend.

'Oh, yes—yes, he does.'

And John had let her go on thinking that the

new heir to Milk River was some grizzled old pro-
spector found roaming somewhere way out in the
Australian outback. If it had not been for the
misconception she had built up in her mind, she
might have recognised Wolfe for who he was, not
gone on in such ignorance. That accounted for her
uncanny feeling that somewhere, somehow, she
had thought she knew him, but, right or not, all she
felt now was resentful and slightly foolish.

So much for not bothering with television at Milk
River. So much for not really looking closely at the
three-quarter profile picture on the dust jacket of
the books she had ordered in and waited to come
round in the library's Bookmobile.

'I'm surprised you want to keep it quiet,' she said
shortly. 'It must be a glamorous life!'

'What? Writing?' He threw back his head and
laughed. 'Whoever gave you that idea?'

Derek had given her that idea—but then,
Lindsey realised with a jolt, Wolfe had been quite
right. Derek had, so far, never written anything.
He said you had to wait for the muse to strike; that
was why the portable typewriter she had loaned
him still stood on a corner of the farmhouse table
gathering dust. He had to be sure he was ready to
begin before he could start on the novel that was
going to make his name.

A novel! Lindsey clutched at it. That must be the
reason for the difference between the two authors
in her life. Wolfe was talking about days of hard,
solitary work, whereas Derek dwelled on royalties
and best-seller lists but Wolfe just dealt in facts for
his travel books. Derek was planning to undertake
a free-flying exercise of his talent and imagination.

But however much she rationalised, the comparison still bothered her. It reminded her of the hours of study she had been obliged to put in to get her degree; hours that had cut her off from boyfriends and the university social life. Unlike Derek, she had found the work hard and challenging. Derek had found it easy, but he had still not got his degree.

'The problem is,' he had remarked contemptuously one day, 'the establishment just won't accept anyone who's too bright to fit into their scheme of things. They just don't know how to cope with a truly original mind!'

Lindsey relaxed. Of course, that must be it! For all the similarity in age and for all his international success, Wolfe Manston–Marc LeBret was not, like Derek, the owner of a truly original mind.

She studied the owner of that less than brilliant intellect as Wolfe put the truck in gear and started down the mile-long drive. The clear-cut profile was incisive against a darkening sky and the fingers on the wheel controlled it with a strong, sure touch. Lindsey shivered. For a second, she had not been able to picture Derek's face.

There was no one when they drove into the yard. By the time they stopped, Jake had not only appeared with an anxious Toller at his heels but was opening Wolfe's door.

'I've washed your car down.' Jake couldn't wait for Wolfe's approval. 'Given her a grease job as well.'

Lindsey got out of the truck unnoticed and walked around the hood.

'Thanks, Jake.' She saw Wolfe smile wryly. 'I'm

sure the rental people will be pleased! And now,'
he glanced down at once immaculate cords, dust-
streaked now from the miles they had walked
across the fields. Seeing everything once removed
had not been enough for him. They had scrambled
down and scrambled back and walked miles to
and from the truck. 'I guess I'd better go in and
change. I'd like to be off before it's completely
dark.'

'But I—we—' Lindsey turned to include Adeline
who had appeared at the kitchen door. 'We thought
you would be staying on!' She had caught herself in
time; she had almost said hoped instead of thought.
But it was Adeline and Jake who hoped; she was
just there to do a job.

Wolfe's voice was expressionless. 'No, I've business to settle in Toronto. I'm booked on the flight
from Saskatoon tonight. What's the problem?' he
asked suddenly. 'Are you worried you won't be
able to manage here on your own for the next few
weeks?'

'Of course not!' She made it sound as ridiculous
as a slight feeling of what she could only identify as
disappointment. He was going for a few weeks, and
the less she had to do with Wolfe Manston for the
next six months, the better. 'Whether you're here
or not, it makes no difference,' she added for good
measure.

'In that case,' in the gathering dusk his face was
hard and hostile, 'you've got nothing to worry
about, have you?'

Lindsey was upstairs at her bedroom window when
he left. She had had no intention of being there, but

she had been drawn by the sound of voices. Jake's, of course, spinning out the last few moments, and the voice of Wolfe himself; laughing and patient, not clipped and slightly hostile.

Wolfe had changed into the dark suit he had worn when she had first seen him and his face was even darker above immaculate white linen. She watched as he got into the car.

She hadn't even said goodbye—let Jake and Adeline say the goodbyes and do all the talking— she had just come upstairs and had a shower. Now she was standing in her robe, watching the car go underneath the yellow yard light and then through the gate and along the drive.

It was a good three-hour drive to Saskatoon and then Wolfe had the flight on to Toronto. A journey of seventeen—eighteen—hundred miles to a world in which Milk River might never have existed. Wolfe had talked in terms of being away for weeks, but why should he ever bother to come back? He had not bothered, after all, to tell her that he was leaving.

Lindsey pulled the curtains on two receding blurs of tail lights and on her own reaction.

'Telephone!' She was halfway down the back stairs, dressed and with her still damp blonde hair pulled back and tied at her neck, when Adeline's head appeared around the kitchen door.

She had no need to be told that her caller must be Derek; she could tell that from the expression on Adeline's face. Like Ben Manston, Adeline had not been impressed. Derek's charm and big city glamour had left her untouched and suspicious, and Lindsey could feel her stony eyes boring into her when she picked up the telephone.

'How did it go?' The farmhouse had no telephone, so Derek must be calling from a pay phone somewhere, wanting to know every detail of her day. No—if she was honest, Derek was much more interested in knowing what, if anything, had been said about the will. It didn't take long to realise that as he went on questioning her.

She heard a loud burst of raucous laughter in the background. Derek must be calling from the hotel in which she and Wolfe had lunched.

'Dammit, I can't talk here!' Derek said crossly. 'If Manston's gone, why don't I come over?'

'Tonight?' Normally she would have jumped at the idea.

'Why not?' He was suspicious. 'Don't you want to see me?'

'Yes, but—' Lindsey wavered. Of course she wanted to see Derek, but not here. Milk River belonged to Wolfe now; its whole ambience had changed. At first it had been the comparison of Wolfe and Ben—not wanting to see a stranger in her uncle's place—now it was the comparison of Derek and Wolfe that bothered her. 'But don't come here.' She rushed it, not giving him a chance for questions or herself for answers. 'Let's go out somewhere. You're at the hotel, aren't you? I'll pick you up outside in twenty minutes. No one'll see us!'

Not being seen together had been the one cloud on her whole relationship with Derek. When she had realised she had fallen in love, she had wanted to shout it from the housetops or, at least, officially announce their engagement in the Saskatoon and local papers, but Derek had been against it, and then her uncle had fallen sick and nothing else had mattered.

So no one knew; not her uncle, Adeline or the sharp eyes in the village. It was one more secret, one more mystery, to add to all the rest.

She felt she could hardly remember a time when life had been clear and simple. First there had been Derek and then the will to cloud and tangle the horizon.

At that moment, she would have given everything to go away. To stop pretending and deceiving and try and start life again, as clear and as untroubled as it had once been. With Derek. Of course, with Derek.

She had her salary; her mind went racing on, finding ways and means. Ben had paid her, insisted on paying her, far more than she could reasonably have expected as an inexperienced ranch manager elsewhere, and Wolfe had mentioned offhandedly during an otherwise silent lunch that he intended to continue paying her the same amount. Most of that, like the rest, would stay in the bank. There was little on which to spend money at Milk River, and the balance in the last statement from the bank about her term deposits had amazed her.

Her uncle had also arranged for the insurance money that had been paid out when her parents had been killed to be safely invested in gilt-edged stocks and shares. That was there, too. The will which had not mentioned her would by no means leave her destitute. Until Derek wrote his book, they could live—maybe modestly, but they could live almost anywhere.

At that moment, staring at the telephone, feeling Adeline's inimical gaze across the kitchen, Lindsey wanted no more than to get out and leave it all behind her. Let Wolfe have his land, his stocks, his shares, his bonds—everything that went with his inheritance to ensure that the name of Manston would survive and that the continuity of Milk River, a continuity which Wolfe had also somehow seemed to sense, would be preserved and she would leave, with Derek, not stay six months to fight a battle in which she had no interest.

'You're going out, then?' Adeline broke the silence.

'Yes—I'm sorry.' Lindsey glanced at pots and pans steaming on the stove. 'Perhaps we can have it cold tomorrow.'

'Perhaps.' Adeline turned a thickened back and the temperature in the kitchen dropped to zero.

Derek was waiting for Lindsey when she pulled up outside the hotel in Annabel, and they went almost to Saskatoon before they found a truck stop-cum-Chinese restaurant in which Derek was sure they would not be recognised.

He *was* Derek—just the same Derek, with a lock of fair curly hair falling across his flushed forehead—but Lindsey found herself studying him as if she had never seen him before. She tested herself to see if the old feelings were still there. Of course they were; blunted, perhaps, in her present frame of mind and by Derek's preoccupation with what he considered the inequity of the will, but there just the same. Waiting to turn into her usual sense of dazed incredulity that someone as handsome and as talented as Derek Foster could ever have given her a second glance.

'Of course you're entitled to something from the will!' Across the formica-topped table and the remains of sweet and sour, Derek was harping on the subject. 'You're the old man's closest relative, after all!'

The offhand way he spoke about her uncle hurt, but then the whole evening had been a series of petty hurts and pinpricks, starting when Lindsey had drawn up outside the hotel in Milk River in Annabel.

Annabel was old, but she belonged to her, whereas both the truck and Ben Manston's Cadillac belonged to the estate—and that meant Wolfe as far as Derek was concerned.

'It's not as if he'd know which car you used,' Derek had exploded angrily. 'He's hundreds of bloody miles away by now!'

Yes, he was. On his way back to his own world, which included neither her nor Milk River. 'But neither of the others belongs to me—' Lindsey started, then she stopped. Derek had already made it clear that he considered her entitled to a share of Ben Manston's will. What point was there in antagonising him further by trying to explain a suddenly deep-rooted thought that she had no right to make a claim? Especially when she scarcely understood that thought herself.

She switched subjects, but in spite of all her efforts, Derek refused to be appeased. He stayed sulky all through the drive and through their Chinese dinner at the truck stop.

Perhaps she should have persuaded him to drive

the extra miles and go on to Saskatoon. Then they could have had their meal at the little French restaurant he liked so much. It was expensive, but it would have been more than worth it if it had changed his mood.

Poor Derek; he missed not having money so very much. When they had first started to go out, Lindsey had been alarmed at the way he paid for everything using one of the many credit cards he seemed to carry, and she had finally persuaded him to let her pay. He could repay her when his book was published, she had argued. Then he would be rich—and famous. She had nothing on which to spend her large salary, whereas Derek only had his tiny annuity on which to live.

He had eventually capitulated under her persuasion, and usually the scheme worked well. She always gave him the money beforehand and he accepted the situation with a good grace. Tonight, however, even though the amount involved had been only a few dollars, he had been bitterly resentful, almost making an angry public scene in the diner for the benefit of the truckers and the Chinese owners, and he was still bad-tempered when they had driven home and he stopped the car outside his isolated farmhouse.

'This is damned ridiculous!' he muttered when Annabel was still juddering to a halt seconds after he had switched off the ignition. 'I still don't see why we couldn't have used your uncle's Caddie!'

Lindsey made a last effort to get him to understand. 'I just wouldn't feel comfortable if we did. I'm sure Wolfe wouldn't mind, but . . .'

'So it's Wolfe already, is it?' Derek cut in with a sneer.

'Darling, you can't possibly be jealous of a name!' Lindsey suddenly felt near to tears at the apparent hopelessness of getting him to understand. 'And anyway,' she suddenly remembered and went on more optimistically, sure that what she had to say would interest him, 'Wolfe Manston's not his only name. Do you know who he is? Marc LeBret!'

Lindsey sat back expectantly, certain that her news would have some effect, but to her surprise, Derek looked quite blank. A budding writer himself—how strange it was that he failed to recognise Wolfe's pseudonym. 'You know,' she went on quickly, brushing the thought aside, 'Marc LeBret, the travel writer. He's been on television.'

Derek's face changed. 'Oh, him!' he said dismissively. 'That pedlar of trash to the masses!'

'Derek!' The violence of his response amazed her. 'He's good! And I'm not the only one to think so—everybody does,' she justified. 'Anyway, I wondered perhaps if he could help you.'

'How?' Derek seemed uneasy.

'Well, he knows everyone in publishing—he must do. I thought perhaps he could help you find a publisher.' It was not what you knew but who you knew, Derek was always saying, but now his full lips compressed to a thin line.

'Show him my manuscript and hand him my ideas on a plate to turn in as his own, is that what you mean?' he enquired scathingly. 'I know you can be naïve, but you must have been born yesterday to suggest a thing like that!'

The contempt in his voice was so apparent that
Lindsey winced, and Derek realised that he had
gone too far. He leaned across behind the wheel
and took her in his arms. 'Honey, I'm sorry!' His
voice was soft as he brushed his lips across her hair.
'But you *are* an innocent, you know! You just don't
realise what a man like that might do. He's used to
getting his own way,' he went on with vehemence,
'that's why I hate the idea of you being there alone
with him. I must have been crazy to let you talk me
into agreeing that you should stay on!'

It was only later, driving home with the pressure
of Derek's goodnight kiss still vivid on her lips, that
Lindsey thought how strange it was that he seemed
to have forgotten that it had been his idea, not hers,
that she should stay on in order to prove some claim
against the estate. But then, she argued, if he hated
the idea so much, it was understandable that he
should have blocked it from his mind.

Moonlight was streaming in through the windows on either side of the rarely used front door
when Lindsey let herself into the house and walked
across the hall towards the wide main staircase. It
was so quiet that the rustle of falling ashes in the
great stone fireplace sounded like an avalanche,
and she glanced across, wondering if it was safe to
leave the fire still smouldering or if it was still
capable of producing a small explosion of sparks to
shower out on the rug.

She had stood in that hearth, she remembered,
on her first Christmas at Milk River, fascinated by a
chimney that really did seem big enough for Santa
Claus. At eight, she no longer believed in him, of
course, but belief was still close enough to take her

across to the hearth to stand in the bed of soft cold
ashes and peer up into the dark void. A tug on one
of the iron footholds, driven in when men, perhaps,
or boys, had gone up to clean the chimney, had
brought a cloud of grit and soot down on her head
and she had gone scurrying out, crying and rubbing
the grit from her eyes, leaving a trail of small black
footprints all across the floor.

That had been the first time Ben Manston must
have realised exactly what taking a child into his
previously ordered bachelor life was going to
mean, and Lindsey smiled sadly at the memory as
she turned towards the stairs. The fire was safe and
she should go to bed.

Her hand was on the newel post when the telephone began to ring, its sound harsh and totally
demanding in the otherwise silent house. She reluctantly retraced her steps. It must be Wolfe; Derek
had no telephone and no one else would call so late.
Wolfe must have remembered something he had
forgotten to tell her. He had arrived in Toronto and
was calling to tell her what it was.

She picked up the receiver from the telephone on
the side table underneath the stairs. 'Milk River,'
she said.

'Is Wolfe Manston there?' It was certainly not
Wolfe's voice coming down the line. It was
a woman, as clear-cut and authoritative as the
shrilling telephone bell.

'No, I'm afraid he's not. I think he's in Toronto.'

'He can't be! I'm calling from Toronto.' The
voice said it as if no other explanation was required.

'As far as I know, that's where he is,' Lindsey
replied.

'You must be wrong.' The voice was adamant. 'If he was here, I'd know. But not to worry,' it went on almost in an aside, 'I don't suppose he tells his staff all his plans. Take a message for him, will you?'

Piqued by the obvious assumption that she was no more than a simple-minded servant with nothing better to do than take telephone messages in the middle of the night, Lindsey fumbled for the message pad and pencil.

'Tell him that Carla Morris called,' the woman's voice forced her to concentrate. 'Tell him to call me at the apartment . . . Damn! What is this wretched number, anyway?' There was a pause while the invisible Carla Morris checked the number at her end and then relayed it. 'Now,' she said, 'you're sure you've got that down? Perhaps you'd better read it back.'

By now thoroughly annoyed, Lindsey repeated the message through tight lips.

'You seem to have got it right, at least.' Carla's confirmation was clearly grudging. 'Now make sure that Mr. Manston gets it as soon as you see him, there's a good girl!' She rang off without a thank you or goodbye, leaving Lindsey at boiling point.

All in all, it had been a thoroughly unsettling evening. First Derek's moody temper and now this Carla Morris's insufferably patronising call. She tried to calm herself.

Derek had been neither moody nor bad-tempered when she left him, and as for Carla Morris, she was entirely Wolfe's concern. If that was the sort of woman with whom he wished to get involved, it was his affair.

Feeling unaccountably depressed and tired, Lindsey left the telephone and started up the staircase to her room.

CHAPTER FOUR

'I'VE dealt with that.' Wolfe flicked the piece of paper with Carla Morris's message into the wastepaper basket beside what had once been Ben Manston's desk and then glanced across at Lindsey. 'Is there anything else?'

'No, I don't think so.' Aware of a quite inexplicable lift of spirit, Lindsey checked her notes. 'Ralph Pinder's due at any minute to discuss the drainage scheme for his ranch. I've contacted the surveyor and he'll be here tomorrow, and the livestock research people are sending the information you wanted me to get.' She ticked off notes she had made during Wolfe's first tour of the ranch. 'And—oh!' She looked up. He was watching her far more closely than seemed necessary. 'I've spoken to Jake about getting the snow fence checked and up earlier this year. Otherwise—' her voice began to tail away. She couldn't concentrate when he looked at her like that. '—I've just got on with my usual work and caught up with what needed to be done.'

She caught a glint of a knowing smile and flushed. But she was good at her job, she knew it. She might not be sophisticated and glamorous—how many times since she had called had her imagination supplied the picture?—like the unknown Carla Morris, but she was good at her job.

They were in the farm office on the far side of the

60

house, and this time Wolfe's arrival had not caught
her by surprise.

Even if there had not been a warning phone call
from someone in an unidentified Toronto office,
she would still have been prepared. Her desk, set at
an angle to her uncle's old one, had been clear for
days and she had been proud of its clean surface.
Her only apprehension was if Wolfe would approve
of everything she had achieved.

Her uncle trusted her, but he had wanted to
know what she was doing every step of the way.
Wolfe, on the other hand, gave instructions and
then left her to carry them out. It produced a novel
and not unwelcome feeling of complete responsibility, but the question of his approval had always
been there, lurking in the background of her mind.

Not that she really cared if he approved or not,
she had tried to convince herself. If he dis-
approved, he could always fire her and make the
decision that she should leave Milk River which she
somehow couldn't bring herself to make herself.

But all the rationalisations in the world hadn't
stopped her feeling nervous when she had heard
the rented car coming up the drive. She had been
upstairs and she had gone across to her bedroom
window, staying carefully behind the curtains as the
car had pulled into the yard. It stopped, the door
opened and Wolfe got out.

Jake was there and so was Toller; even Adeline
had managed to be walking across the yard with her
morning bowl of corn for her chickens, but from the
moment the car door opened, Lindsey saw only
Wolfe.

He was no closer than the others. There was no

reason for him to blot them out or seem more vital and clear-cut in the bright November sunshine. It was also impossible that he could see her, no one could see through a window into an unlit room from a distance of fifty feet, but in that moment, Wolfe's dark head had turned and grey eyes had looked straight at her. Lindsey had drawn back behind her protective curtain and gone downstairs to the farm office. She was imagining things, she must be, but his footsteps in the corridor had still made her stomach jump and her hand go up to smooth her already smoothed-back hair. And why shouldn't she be nervous? she asked herself. It was the first time she had been left to run Milk River by herself.

'You say Pinder's coming over?'

'Yes.' She had absorbed the shock of seeing him by now. Of realising that he was not the same but more than she remembered. 'I told him that you want to drain the slough and—' she no longer had to look to see the steady, level eyes or the strong lines of the face, '—he wants to talk it over.'

'Really?' He sounded questioning. He wanted an explanation, but she stayed looking at her notes. There was silence, then a hand and arm came out and fingers started to riffle through the pile of papers on the desk. 'Remind me to give you power of attorney to sign contracts.'

'Oh, why?' Lindsey kept her voice as cool as his.

'Because I'm leaving.'

'Leaving?' Her voice rose and her head went back before she could stop herself.

'I'm going to Toronto.' Had he seen the effect his news had had on her? Surely not. His face was half turned away in profile and he was frowning as he re-read a letter on the desk. 'My publishers want a coffee-table book using some of the photographs I brought back from Australia,' he elaborated without looking up, 'and it's more convenient for me to work there.'

And closer to the unknown Carla, a spiteful inner imp supplied. Not that she was interested in his personal relationships—male or female. To her, remote kinship notwithstanding, he was no more than a man whom circumstance had cast in the role of her employer. Why else would she have struggled to keep the atmosphere so formal since he had come in through the door and she had watched his smile die under the chilliness of her greeting?

'I'll be away for a few weeks,' he continued shortly.

So he *was* coming back. More than angry, Lindsey despised herself. Here she was, telling herself that what he did and where he went could not be of less interest, and yet her heart was leaping.

'I'm catching the plane back tomorrow.' This time he couldn't possibly have noticed. Both voice and eyes were frigid. 'Before I go, however, I'd like to ride across and take a second look at that farmhouse we're renting out.'

Lindsey went numb. 'Which farmhouse?' she queried woodenly.

'I wasn't aware we were renting more than one!' Wolfe's voice was thin and he leaned back in his chair; no doubt now that he watching her. 'While I'm talking things over with Pinder, you might tell Jake to get the horses ready.'

'Of course!' Lindsey made a totally unnecessary note and felt the blood returning to her cheeks. She had no need to be so apprehensive. Wolfe wanted to meet Derek, that was all, and what could be more natural than a landlord wanting to meet his last tenant—even if that tenant had not paid his rent in quite a while. They were not expected to be friendly or fall into each other's arms—and although Derek was already antagonistic towards a man he had never met, Wolfe could be much colder. She could feel a chill touching her across the office. A meeting was hardly likely to develop into the sort of lengthy conversation in which the matter of the unpaid rent, or her efforts to cover it, would casually be disclosed. Nor was her uncle's will, the reason—the only reason—why she was staying on, likely to crop up.

No, Lindsey convinced herself, Wolfe and Derek would have the sort of formal conversation landlords usually did have with their tenants and then she and Wolfe would leave with her and Derek's secrets still intact.

If only she could call Derek and forewarn him. Her sudden wishful thinking made a mockery of her efforts to rationalise her fears about the meeting. But farmhouses that did not have running water did not have telephones.

'Incidentally,' Wolfe cut in to her train of thought, 'why's Pinder coming to see me? I thought you were going to see him and deal with that.'

'I did—see him, I mean.' But it was a man's world at Milk River. Was she ever going to be able to stop saying that? Not while the man who owned it was facing her in his chair, half leaning back, hands thrust into the pockets of charcoal worsted trousers and his head bent slightly above the dark wool shirt as he studied her beneath straight eyebrows. Had he ever smiled? Lindsey looked at the dark compression of his mouth. It seemed impossible.

'So?' Wolfe prompted.

What had happened when she had gone across to see Ralph Pinder and explained Wolfe's plan to drain the slough that made fifty acres of arable land impossible to cultivate was that Ralph had refused to take her seriously. A scheme that size had to be explained man to man before it was acceptable; not by old Ben Manston's niece, even with her fancy degree in agriculture. Lindsey had tried and Ralph had listened—she was, after all, the old boss's kin—but then he had walked away, telling her to call him and let him know when he could come and speak to Wolfe, the new boss.

Lindsey relived the sheer frustration of mounting Fire Bird and riding angrily away. She now lived the acute unwillingness of having to explain to Wolfe.

'He wasn't too clear . . .' she began, but then she heard footsteps coming along the corridor and broke off, relieved. 'But that must be Ralph now,' she said hastily. 'Why don't you let him explain?' Things would be no better, but at least she need not be there to hear.

She got up and opened the door. Ralph's face greeted her. He wasn't pleased, that much was obvious as he stood there in green coveralls and a duck-billed canvas cap, colourless from the dust of several harvests. Lindsey had never seen him without that cap. She wondered sometimes if he went to bed in it.

'Ma'am!' He touched the peak. 'Your Indian woman said the boss was here.'

'Yes, he is.' Lindsey stood back to let him see Wolfe at the desk. 'Excuse me,' she said, 'I'll go and get some coffee.'

There was no answer. Fetching coffee was just something women did.

She had to stop reacting in this way. Stop feeling as resentful as she did that, when she got back to the farm office with her loaded coffee tray, a plan that had been totally unacceptable when she had struggled to explain it had now been whole-heartedly embraced. Ralph was even willing to help her get it carried out—as Wolfe's deputy.

'Call me if those fellows in Saskatoon start giving you any hassle,' he said solemnly, 'and *I'll* have a word with them!'

A suspicious, resistant Westerner had walked into the office; a totally converted ally left.

'You handled him well.' Lindsey heard her grudging admiration.

Wolfe did not look up. 'Why not? I'm a Manston!' *Now* he looked up and eyes like cold grey comet tails flicked over her. 'If that's everything here, I'd better go and get changed if we're going to ride over to the old Kersey place—but before I do,' he stopped in the act of rising from his chair, 'you'd better have this in case you want to get in touch with me while I'm away.' He pulled a pad towards him and wrote quickly in a boldly slanted hand. 'It's my Toronto address and telephone number.' He tore the sheet off the pad and gave it to her. 'Put it somewhere safe.'

He left her standing staring at the address of an apartment block, presumably in downtown Toronto, with a telephone number underneath. The address meant nothing, but the telephone number did. It was the one the unknown Carla Morris had left when she had called. She could hardly be mistaken, particularly as Carla had made her repeat it.

Jake was missing when Lindsey got out into the yard and she got the horses ready herself.

Turpin, her uncle's stallion, gave her a sidelong look that showed the whites of his eyes as she banged the cold saddle on to his back with unnecessary force and Fire Bird, in the next stall in the barn, skittered uneasily across the straw as she led Turpin past and out through the door. She looped his reins over a hook on the wall and went back for Fire Bird.

She didn't care, she really didn't care who shared Wolfe's apartment—or his telephone. She tightened Fire Bird's girth with a jerk that made the mare lash out with a hind leg. The fact that Wolfe was living with Carla couldn't concern her less, nor was she in the least upset about Wolfe making the excuse of having a book to finish so that he could get back to her. His eagerness, after all, was entirely his affair!

She, after all, had Derek, and the only reason she was staying on at all at Milk River was to prove her claim to some share in the estate. A share her uncle would most certainly have wanted her to have if his illness had not struck with such a crippling swiftness and there had been time for him to have another will drawn up.

What was strange, though, was that Wolfe had not brought Carla to Milk River with him. She would have thought he would have wanted to show the woman he loved the place that was to be her future home. Although eyebrows would be raised in this still old-fashioned part of the world at the thought of an unmarried man and woman living together, Wolfe was clearly not a man to be concerned with gossip or what other people thought. Besides, he lived by Toronto standards where such extra-marital arrangements were commonplace, especially in the artistic set in which he and Carla doubtless moved.

But on her way out of the barn with Fire Bird, Lindsey went cold. Perhaps there was a reason why Carla had not come back with him, and perhaps that reason was that Wolfe planned to sell.

It was awful and unthinkable, but the more she thought it through, the more logical it became.

So much for his talk about the Manston name and about his feeling for the continuity of Milk River. Wolfe might well be touched—might well have his regrets—but if he wanted Carla, perhaps he had no choice.

The owner of the cool, sophisticated voice she had heard coming down the telephone did not sound like the sort of person who would be willing to bury herself in the depths of the Canadian prairies. It was a voice for the bright lights, theatres and smart restaurants of Toronto, and unless Wolfe wanted to run the risk of losing Carla, Toronto could well be where he *had* to live.

Of course he had his obligations. He would hardly be able to sell until all the legal ramifications of his inheritance had been clarified, but that was no reason why he shouldn't start on improvements, such as draining the land Ralph Pinder farmed. Improvements like that would only make Milk River an even better prospect when the time did come to sell.

How fortunate Wolfe must have thought himself when the penniless, dependent relative he had probably expected had turned out to be not just qualified but competent to run the ranch while he went back to his mistress and made his plans to sell. And if she hadn't recognised the telephone number he had given her as the one that Carla left, she would never have suspected anything.

The thought took away any last vestige of guilt she might have had about staying on just to prove some claim to her uncle's will. Not only would she stay, but in case her suspicions were correct, she would take the first opportunity she could to see her uncle's lawyer and find out if there was any way a sale could be blocked.

It was a cold day for riding—a day for sheepskin coats and heavy gloves—but Lindsey was flushed and sitting ramrod-straight on Fire Bird's back when Wolfe came out into the yard.

He, too, had his sheepskin coat, but he had changed into tight, leg-fitting jeans and pointed cowboy boots, and somewhere he had found a wide-brimmed hat belonging to Ben Manston. He came towards her, head bent and pulling on leather gloves, and for a second, it was her uncle coming across the yard.

He looked up, and all similarity instantly vanished to be replaced by a far more dangerous response that Lindsey angrily beat down. *Nothing* about Wolfe Manston was going to impress her. Not his looks, his force, not even that dangerously deceptive air he had of belonging.

She dug her heels into Fire Bird's flanks and tugged Turpin towards him.

'Thanks!' Wolfe took the reins, turned the heavy wooden stirrup towards his toe and swung himself up into the high Western saddle. Turpin reacted and Wolfe controlled him with a flexing of thigh muscles. 'Where's Jake?' He was looking round the yard as the big horse settled, sure of his mastery in the saddle.

'I've no idea.' Lindsey spoke through tightened lips. In fact, she knew Jake was out putting up snow fences, but it gave her satisfaction to plead ignorance.

Wolfe's eyebrows rose, but she bent her head between her own hat and the collar of her sheepskin coat and turned Fire Bird's head towards the gate, leading the way out of the yard without another word.

It had been a day of blue and gold earlier that morning, but the weather had changed in sympathy with her mood. Heavy cloud was coming in over the hills rimming the horizon and the sun had disappeared. Snow was already on the ground; some of it would melt, but the rest would stay, ready to form the base of frozen white for winter storms which would change the whole contour of the land.

'How long have we got to get the drainage

scheme at Pinder's under way?' Wolfe's voice came from behind her, above the sound of hooves and creak of leather.

'Not long. Maybe it'll even have to wait till spring. The land surveyor will have a better idea when he comes tomorrow.'

Turpin's head appeared beside her elbow, then his neck and shoulders with a gloved hand holding the reins lightly above his withers. Lindsey refused to look further than that hand.

They rode past the slough and up the swale in silence.

'Have the surveyor take a look at the house as well while he's here, will you?'

Lindsey looked across. 'Why?' He looked so right, riding her uncle's horse, but she was immediately suspicious. Wasn't having a survey done the first stage of preparation for a sale?

'See for yourself!' Wolfe reined Turpin in and twisted in the saddle. The house lay beneath them under its roof of silvered cedar shakes. 'Look along the ridge,' Wolfe instructed. 'Some of the shakes have slipped and fallen. Get the surveyor to have a look at it, and while he's here, he might as well give the whole place a thorough check. And before you ask why again,' he cut through drily, 'stop and ask yourself when it was last done!'

Lindsey flushed. It shouldn't be so easy for him to second guess her. And why had she not noticed? She had ridden up and down this swale a million times, and yet it had had to be Wolfe who had noticed the poor state of the roof on his first time out. 'Never, I think,' she answered shortly.

'Then get it done!' he answered. 'I don't want to

be remembered as the Manston who neglected his inheritance!'

No—just sold it!

Wolfe touched his heels to Turpin's flanks and the big horse bounded forward. Lindsey followed. Why shouldn't he want to put the house in good repair? she argued. It would be an expensive undertaking—once started there were probably other things that needed to be done—but, once again, from the point of view of making a good sale it was no more than a profitable investment.

'Which way do we go?' Wolfe's voice reached her through the wind and thudding hooves.

'What?' Lindsey jerked her mind from the future to the present.

'Which way is it to the old Kersey place?' Wolfe shot her a sideways glance through dark lashes.

'Oh!' Derek! She had forgotten. For a moment, she lost the horse's rhythm and Fire Bird snatched peevishly at the reins. 'It's over there.' She jerked her head in the direction of a thin plume of smoke rising from a chimney hidden behind a patch of stunted bush.

'Okay—fine!' Wolfe veered slightly and Fire Bird followed, beginning to race the other horse. Lindsey made no attempt to stop her. She could see the roof of Derek's rented farmhouse now, behind Wolfe's moving shoulder, but beyond that, nothing; just snowbound prairie, empty like her future, beneath a steel-grey sky like the underside of a flat iron.

Riding mindlessly, she wallowed in a curious mixture of anger and self-pity. As if finding out about Wolfe's plans wasn't enough to handle for

one morning, she now had his first meeting with
Derek to get through.

Wolfe's rhythmically moving back went past and
dropped behind her. Fire Bird was galloping now,
but she pushed her faster, not caring that the wind
had snatched her hat and that her hair was streaming out behind her. Wolfe shouted, but she ignored
him. What was happening was his fault. Derek
could not be blamed for persuading her to stay on at
Milk River. He could not have known that, by
staying, she would have to stand aside and watch it
sold around her. And Derek could certainly not be
blamed for the sudden reawakening of all her fears
about the two men meeting.

What comparison could there be between
Derek, the man she loved, and Wolfe, the man she
hated?

Like most farmhouses, the old Kersey place had
been built in a slight hollow to protect it from the
wind, and as Fire Bird hit the slope, she began to
slip and slither, uncertain of her footing on the
semi-frozen surface and alarmed. Lindsey tried,
but Fire Bird was past stopping, driven on by
sudden panic and the sound of hoofbeats coming up
fast behind them.

'You're going to kill yourself one day if you go on
like this!' A hand and then an arm came out, then
Wolfe was there beside them, leaning forward in an
easy, fluid movement to catch the reins and bring
the snorting, frenzied quarter horse to a stop.

'Thank you!' The moment she regained her
balance, Lindsey wrenched the reins away. 'And
that, I suppose, would be highly inconvenient,' she
gasped out through painful, sobbing breaths. 'If

you lost your ranch manager, you'd have to find someone else to run Milk River!'

'Is that really all you think you mean to me?' He should have been annoyed or joking; he should have been anything except as suddenly serious as he was.

Lindsey felt the first flickering of a different sort of apprehension and, in that moment, the horses moved, bringing them much closer until no more than inches separated their set faces. She could feel his breath against her cheek and see her own reflection, and the awful thought went through her head that she wanted him to kiss her.

She leaned towards him, dry lips parted, and watched his face reflect the shadow of her longing. In a second his mouth would be against hers and she would know what lay beneath the surface of those probing eyes.

The scream of tyres on gravel cut through the moment. Fire Bird reared, startled by the sudden and unusual noise, and by the time Lindsey had controlled her, Wolfe was watching a heavy black car racing down the laneway from the farmhouse.

'Someone in a hurry to get away!' He turned to her with no more than casual interest written on his face.

Had she dreamed those last few moments, or had they really taken place?

The car accelerated and then braked to take the turn out of the side road, fishtailing violently before the driver regained control and then disappearing in the direction of the main highway, leaving only the sound of its powerful engine hanging in the air.

Had she felt Wolfe reaching out to touch her, or had his longing been only in her mind?

'Your author friend?' Wolfe's ironic smile offered just one answer—that she had been a fool.

'No, I don't think so.' She could also pretend that nothing had ever taken place. Besides, she was puzzled. Not only had the man hunched over the steering wheel of the car not been Derek, he hadn't looked in the least like any of the artistic Toronto friends about whom Derek was always talking. In fact, if anything, this man had looked more like a heavyweight boxer than an actor or a writer; she had caught a glimpse of close cropped hair on a heavy, bullet-shaped head.

'Oh, well, let's go and see if Foster's there.' Along with her, Wolfe had also lost interest in the car. But Foster—Foster? Lindsey frowned. She was sure she had never mentioned Derek's name; that would have been dangerous ground, taking her too close to other truths. 'If he is,' Lindsey stopped worrying the small mystery, 'he'll certainly be awake—our racing driver friend made enough noise to wake the dead!'

Wolfe ended the discussion and they rode past the barns towards the house in an awkward silence.

'I see your friend's no gardener!' Wolfe swung down from the saddle and patted Turpin's neck, taking in the neglected patch of ground beside the house, growing nothing but tin cans and paper. 'Will he stand?'

'Yes, they both will.' Lindsey also dismounted and dropped the open-ended reins on the ground beside Fire Bird's feet. Wolfe copied her and Turpin rested a hind leg. 'And no—I told you, he's an author, not a gardener.' She still felt awkward about using Derek's name.

Wolfe smiled. 'An author who has yet to write a book!'

'That's not fair!' Her defence was much too fast and vehement, and Lindsey turned away, anxious once more to get the encounter over; anxious to get away.

The farmhouse looked both desolate and neglected. No one cared, and no one had since the first Wolfe had bought the Kerseys out, and Derek was the last person to be concerned about his surroundings—the papers and cans thrown in the garden and the dirt and dust inside. It was strange that, coming from a wealthy background, Derek took so little interest in how he lived, but then, when he had been growing up, his parents had had servants and creative, artistic people were notorious for their lack of interest in appearances.

Lindsey knocked on the screen door, knowing as she did so that there was no one there. The knock had a hollow, empty sound which even the presence of one person in a house will change, but Lindsey went on waiting, keeping her back to Wolfe.

He must be the exception to the rule about artistic people and appearance. She selfconsciously pushed her own tangled fair hair back and made a mental note to retrieve the hat that she had lost on her wild ride. Even now, even after that wild gallop, Wolfe looked as he always did—hard, clearcut, with the fine grain of his skin dark against the fleecy whiteness of his collar.

She raised her hand to knock again.

'Don't bother!' Wolfe, slightly behind her, dismissed her effort. 'If that car didn't rouse him, nothing will. Foster's obviously not here. Just get someone to clear this mess away.' He cut through her guilty feeling of relief that all meetings and comparisons had been postponed. 'What do you get round here—' he glanced towards the bush and the open prairie, '—bears? Skunks? Whatever it is, we don't want to give them an open invitation! And now we'd better get back—it looks like snow.'

They mounted and rode silently away under a sky that went greyly on for ever. In a week or two, the snow sprinkled land around them would be white with snow, ready to blow southward at knee height in the first strong wind. A blizzard destroyed all sense of direction, making a featureless land even more featureless, and the arrival of those blizzards would mark not only the beginning of the first winter Lindsey had spent at Milk River without Ben Manston, it could also mark the ending of the ranch itself as she had always known it if she was right in thinking what its new owner had in mind.

She glanced across at him. Under the pulled-down brim of his hat, his face was dark and brooding, offering no hint of what might be going through his head, but if she could not read his thoughts, he could not read hers.

He could have no idea that, if he did have plans to sell Milk River, she was going to fight him all the way.

CHAPTER FIVE

JAKE stopped Wolfe in the yard when they got back and Adeline was missing from the kitchen, so Lindsey was alone when she pushed open the swing door leading from the rear part of the house into the main hall. Alone and in the same mood of gritty determination in which she had ridden home. She would not let Wolfe destroy Milk River and all it stood for. She would not!

The air trapped in the swing of the door behind her broke the silence with a long sigh and a figure hunched up on the couch beside the fire looked up.

Lindsey caught her breath and strained her eyes. Surely the house was empty! The hall faced north and the weather outside made it unnaturally dark. The lights were off and it was hard to see, but then the figure moved and it was Derek. Derek with a whisky decanter and a half empty glass on the end table beside the sofa. Lindsey let out her breath with a long rush of relief mixed, an instant later, with alarm. With Derek here and Wolfe outside but coming in at any minute, the meeting she thought had been avoided was now bound to take place.

'Lin!' Derek scrambled unsteadily to his feet and Lindsey forgot all about the meeting as he stumbled, half running, across the hall towards her. His face was white and drawn, lacking all trace of its usual self-assurance, and when he got to her and took her arm, drawing her from the even darker gloom underneath the stairs into the circle of half light cast by the fire, his fingers transmitted the touch of physical fear.

'Lin, thank God you've come!' Even his voice was different; lacking its usual expensive private school overtones.

'Derek, what's wrong?' She had never seen him like this before. He was frightened; the word 'hunted' flashed across her mind. 'Derek, what's the matter?'

He gripped her arm urgently. 'I've got to get away from here,' he muttered. 'Now—today!'

'What do you mean—get away? Do you mean you want us to go off somewhere and get married?' Lindsey was surprised, but not as surprised as she might have been. Soon after they first met, Derek had suggested they elope, saying that any resistance her uncle might have to their marriage would be overcome by an established fact. Lindsey had been doubtful and, sensing her reluctance, Derek had laughed the idea away, saying he was teasing. But if he had been teasing then, he was in deadly earnest now.

'Sure, we'll get married if you like.' It seemed as if having her in his arms was making him feel safer. He was beginning to recover his composure and, with it, his normal educated voice. 'We'll do anything so that we can go somewhere together and be alone! I want you, Lin!' He held her close and looked down at her until all she was aware of was the handsome face and the watchful blue intensity of his eyes. 'You just don't know how much I hate the thought of you being here, alone—with him!' His face came closer.

'If it's not too much trouble, perhaps you could introduce us!' The mocking voice with the razor edge came from the shadows underneath the stairs. Derek froze with his lips just touching hers, and Lindsey pulled herself from his arms.

She turned towards the shadows—and then she also froze. Wolfe had come in unnoticed and was standing there, smiling with a smile that left his eyes untouched. She immediately felt embarrassed and at a loss—and yet why should she? She was over twenty-one and no one, certainly not Wolfe, had the right to choose her friends or say who she should see. Drawing the flimsy protection of the thought around her, she stood her ground to face Wolfe as he came closer.

'Derek Foster—Wolfe Manston.' Her lips were trembling.

The two men faced each other, making no effort to shake hands—Derek tall and fair and Wolfe dark, with his muscular compactness making him seem slighter. Why, then, did all the impression of power and authority in the room rest with the slighter man?

'Ah, the elusive Mr Foster!' Wolfe cut through Lindsey's uncomfortable little insight with a rasping drawl she had never heard before. 'I've been looking forward to making your acquaintance, although I hardly expected when I did that it would be in my house when you were making yourself so much at home with my property!' He looked pointedly past Lindsey towards the whisky decanter on the end table by the couch.

Derek began to bluster. 'Look here,' he said, 'it's Lin's home as well, or had you forgotten that?'

'No, I hadn't.' Wolfe's icy calmness only served to accentuate Derek's rapidly slipping control. 'What I hadn't realised, however, is that her friends appear to think they can not only come in as and when they choose but use it as they like!'

'That's not fair!' Lindsey slipped her arm through Derek's. The unconscious gesture placed her on his side and she saw Wolfe's face go hard.

'And not true, either.' With her arm through his, Derek was suddenly more confident. 'Not when a perfect stranger can appear on the scene and take everything that should belong to Lin!'

'I had no hand in drawing up the conditions of the inheritance, if that's what you're talking about,' returned Wolfe. 'They were set long before any of us were born, and although you may find it difficult to believe,' Lindsey watched the thin mouth twist, 'the consequences came as just as much of a shock to me as I'm sure they did to you!'

'Oh, I'm sure!' Derek missed the last part of Wolfe's sentence. 'We all know what a shock it must be to wake up one morning and discover you've inherited a place worth millions, to say nothing of all the cash!'

'So that's what bothers you, is it?' Wolfe's eyes went to their clasped hands. 'Cash?'

'Maybe.' Derek looked down defensively. 'But if you were any sort of gentleman,' he once more gathered pace, 'you would know that Lin deserves her share.'

'Really?' Wolfe refused to be abashed. 'And if you were any sort of businessman, you would know that the estate needs every dime it's got if it's going to survive. What is there?' he changed to a different tack. 'Milk River itself, four smaller ranches; this house, the others—including one, I believe, that we rent out.' Lindsey reacted. So, she felt, did Derek. 'It should all be making money, not losing it hand over fist. It needs capital pumping into it, and new ideas, and that's precisely what I plan to do.'

'But Uncle Ben was always spending money on improvements!' Lindsey found her voice at last. 'He was talking about draining Matt Pinder's slough just before he died!'

'Talking but not doing.' Wolfe was frank and brutal. 'Nothing's changed here in years. Milk River's not just old-fashioned, it's almost feudal!' Another way of saying it was a man's world, *this* man's world, Lindsey reflected as Wolfe switched his attention from her back to Derek. 'And it and anyone can kick and scream as much as they damn well like,' his look was pointed, 'but that's where the money's going. To bring this place right into the twentieth century and turn it into a profitable business.'

Lindsey saw Derek sneer. 'How very nice! And how convenient that you can use money that should be Lin's to do it with! They have a word for that where I come from, you know. It's theft!'

The silence that descended was absolute. Even the fire was still, as if unwilling to draw attention to itself by as much as the rustle of a single ash. Her hand still clasping Derek's and her arm through his, Lindsey watched the darkness of cold anger wipe all expression from Wolfe's face. He took a step towards them; Derek blenched and his fingers tightened on her arm.

'I think,' he said, 'you'd better leave!'

'Now see here . . . !' Derek began to bluster.

'Derek, please!' Lindsey unwound her fingers and slipped her arm through his.

'Okay.' Derek gave in. 'But only if *you're* sure,' he emphasised with a venomous look away at Wolfe. 'I don't trust him here alone with you any more than I trust him in any other way!'

Lindsey saw the muscles clench as Wolfe restrained himself. 'Derek, please!' she urged. 'I'll be fine!'

'Okay, okay, I'll go. But if this so-called gentleman as much as touches you . . .' he began to threaten.

'Stop talking like a character from a third-rate melodrama and get out!' The force of Wolfe's voice sent Derek to the door, but once there, he paused before he opened it.

'I'll see you later, honey,' he promised huskily.

'Get out!' Wolfe took a step towards him and Derek went, leaving utter silence until the fire began to crackle in the draught he had let in, filling the tension-laden atmosphere with an unnaturally loud noise.

Wolfe turned away. 'It's difficult to tell what he's more interested in!' he remarked with a short laugh. 'You, or any possible financial expectations you might still have from the estate!'

His comment touched Lindsey on the raw. 'That's quite ridiculous!' she blazed.

'Is it?' He turned back and studied her with an almost clinical detachment.

'Of course.' She muttered it to the floor.

'Then why is he making use of you?'

Her head went back. 'Making use of me? Derek's not making use of me!'

'He loves you for yourself, is that what you're telling me?' Now there was no mistaking his contempt. 'How convenient for him, then, that you also happen to be the one person with the authority to let him live rent-free!'

'Oh!' Lindsey was shocked. 'I didn't know you knew!'

'Then you're not as intelligent as I thought you were!' Wolfe snapped. 'You don't imagine I could spend several hours with the books and miss a thing like that, do you? I also noticed that the charming Mr Foster stopped paying rent just about the time your uncle got sick and you took over running things—a coincidence that seemed significant!' He walked slowly back and studied her, and it took every ounce of willpower to look him squarely in the eye. 'Do you want to tell me why?' he asked. 'Or can I guess?'

'Because Derek has no money!' He had no right to question her about her private life. 'But he will have,' she flashed defensively, 'just as soon as he writes his book.'

'His book!' Wolfe laughed derisively. 'I realise love is expected to be blind—' so much for trying to hide what Derek meant to her! '—but surely even you can't still believe in that? The man's a charlatan! A fifth-rate character, incapable of writing a fifth-rate novelette, far less a book!'

'How dare you say that!' Anger brought her close to tears. 'Derek's got a brilliant mind!' She had to believe in that, she had to! Wolfe had lanced the growing doubts she had also had, bringing them to

the surface of her mind until they could no longer
be ignored. But, once more, she had to turn her
back on them, she just had to, otherwise how could
she believe that Derek loved her? If he was lying
about his book, he could be lying about his love,
and without that to cling to, she would once more
be as she had always been.

Ordinary and unremarkable Lindsey Kinsale,
living at the big house at Milk River, but now with
one big difference. Now she no longer even had her
uncle, just the man still watching her with obvious
doubt and scepticism written in his face.

'Can you really be as naïve as you pretend, or is it
just an act?' There was no mistaking the derision in
his voice but then his whole face changed. 'Let's
find out, shall we?' he demanded suddenly.

Before she had a chance to guess what he intended, he had caught her by the shoulders and
pulled her to him savagely.

'No!' Her hands went up and she struck out
against the muscle of his chest, but his mouth came
down to cover hers and she was lost.

Her mind was cool and clear and functioning, but
the moment his lips touched hers, her body began
to melt. It was as if someone had lit a fire at every
point they touched. Hips, thighs, breasts, they all
responded to the pressure as Wolfe bent her to him
and his lips began to move with a skilled persuasion. Somehow her fingers were buried in his hair,
feeling its crisp darkness with the last of her reeling
senses, and somehow her mouth was opening
under his. In the darkness behind her lids, blood
pulsed a vivid crimson and she hung there in his
arms as the fever reached her mind and nothing

mattered except her hunger for the man who held her in his arms.

'So!' Suddenly there was distance, no sound except the erratic rhythm of their breathing and no warmth except that coming from the fire. Wolfe smiled—a drawing back of lips from glinting teeth—and suddenly Lindsey understood.

'So,' his drawl was obvious, 'now that we've proved you've got at least some of the responses of a normal adult female, let me ask you the same question!' Lips whose pressure she could still feel were wryly twisted beneath hard, assessing eyes. 'Can you really expect me to believe that you're so innocent you don't know that Foster's making use of you?'

'How dare you?' She struggled to think of something to blot out the memory of those last few seconds. The memory of his heart against her, beating in unison with hers. 'How dare you accuse me of being naïve and stupid,' words in a ragged, breathless flow took over, 'and how dare you accuse anyone of deception when all the time you're planning to sell Milk River?'

Her accusation echoed round the darkened, fire-lit room, each syllable hard and certain. For a moment, something—anger?—contradiction?—flared in Wolfe's veiled eyes, but then all expression vanished and the only thing that counted was the nature of his thin, sardonic smile.

'I won't ask you how you've arrived at that conclusion, but if you prefer to think I plan to sell my heritage rather than face the truth, then there's no more to be said.' He spoke quite calmly, making no attempt to deny what she had said. 'However,' even so, the line around his mouth was white, 'I'm sure I have no need to tell you that your *friend*,' he emphasised the word, 'will not be welcome under this roof while it does continue to be mine. And when you see him, as I'm sure you will,' he taunted, 'perhaps you would also be good enough to tell him that I expect my tenants to pay their rent!'

He turned away, leaving her with only his rigid back to watch as he went up the stairs and disappeared in the direction of what had once been her uncle's room.

Lindsey stood there, not knowing who she hated most, herself or him or the unknown Carla. She suddenly remembered Carla. How dared Wolfe make love to her when he had Carla, and how could she have been such a fool as to respond?

She tried to blot out everything—everything with the exception of one thing: Wolfe's refusal to deny her accusation that he was going to sell the ranch. Until then, selling had only been a supposition, based on a guess. Now, however, it was established fact, as real as the lingering pressure of his mouth against her own.

She bit her lip, trying to produce a different pressure and willing memory to fade. She refused to be affected by a calculated ruse designed to destroy her loyalty to Derek and blind her to Wolfe's plans. Those few moments in his arms had released more than what Wolfe had called the responses of a normal adult female. They had turned guesswork into fact.

CHAPTER SIX

'THERE'S no reason why he can't sell if he wants to—it's up to him.'

Two days later, sitting across the desk from her uncle's lawyer, Lindsey tasted the sourness of defeat. She need not have bothered to come to Saskatoon. She could have stayed home at Milk River and found this out. Instead, she had telephoned for an appointment the moment Wolfe had left and driven Annabel fast into the bridge city.

In contrast to her grey mood of depression, the storm that had grounded planes and kept Wolfe at the ranch for an extra day had left a morning of clear-cut gold behind it, and the South Saskatchewan river she could see outside the window was coated with its first thin sheet of ice.

Wolfe must be somewhere in that pale blue sky above the river, already heading east. Lindsey had gone almost furtively back into the house to telephone for her appointment the moment he had driven out of the yard some four hours earlier. In the time it would take her to drive the same road to Saskatoon in Annabel, Wolfe would be well on his way back to Toronto and his mistress.

The thought had stopped her feeling furtive and bolstered her urge to fight. She had no loyalty to Wolfe. He was a stranger—a cold, unfeeling stranger whom she had done her best to avoid the previous day, denying the treachery of moments when she had found herself reliving the pressure of his mouth against hers and the coarse vibrance of his hair between her fingers.

'I'm not sure when I'll be back.' Slightly ahead of his little entourage of Jake and Adeline and Toller, Wolfe had almost flung it at her as he walked towards his car. 'If there are any problems, call me. You know where I'll be.'

Oh, yes, she knew. He would be with Carla; laughing, perhaps, about her and about the strange old-fashioned world which the accident of sex and birth had dropped into his hands.

'You can send me a written report each week—and,' he paused in the act of pulling on leather gloves, nothing casual about him now, 'make sure Foster gets his rent up to date. I hadn't forgotten, if that's what you were hoping. Do it, Lindsey' he added sharply, 'and do it soon!'

'I'd almost forgotten what it was like to have a man around the place!' Adeline, her Adeline, had not just switched loyalties, she was as moist around the eyes as Toller as Wolfe edged the powerful sports car past a beaming Jake and drove out of the yard.

Damn! Damn, damn, damn! Lindsey had turned and gone back into the house. Would Wolfe be as wonderful if Adeline guessed he could be planning to sell her home?

'There's no legal reason why he can't.' Reality in the form of John's voice brought her back to the present of the book-lined lawyer's office. John was offering her his sympathy; what he was not offering her was doubt. 'He wouldn't be able to for a few months, of course, until all the legal ramifications of his ownership are sorted out, but there's nothing in the entailment to prevent a sale. I guess no one ever thought about it happening, which is why nothing to stop it was ever written in.'

'I see.' Of course no one had ever thought about it happening. No one had ever foreseen that one day there would be no more sons, just the daughter of a daughter and a Manston with a worldwide reputation as an author in another name, who had been summoned from halfway across that world to an inheritance which, apart from a passing sentiment, meant nothing to him.

Lindsey slumped back in her chair. In her heart of hearts, in spite of everything, she had been hoping there was something she could do; some legal avenue open to block a sale. Now she knew. There was nothing.

She listened with only half her mind as John went on explaining in his usual, easy non-legal way. John Miller was one of the new breed of lawyers, not much older than Lindsey was herself and blunt and to the point. When he explained a situation, you knew just where you stood and were not left mystified by the finer legal points. Ben Manston had appreciated his direct approach, and when John had set up on his own, Ben had gone with him.

The transfer of such an important client had helped establish him, and John was grateful. More than that, he and his wife Jan, had become close friends. That was why he knew Lindsey well enough to stop now, sensing her state of complete and utter hopelessness.

'Cheer up! It mightn't be as bad as you think. You've admitted you've got absolutely no proof that he intends to sell, and what was said was said in anger, after all. He certainly gave no indication when he was here that he might be planning to sell. In fact, he was talking more about how to bring the whole place up to date.' John paused, suddenly indecisive. 'Oh, well,' he shrugged, 'I guess there's no harm in telling you if it goes no further, but he's instructed me to release quite a lot of his own personal capital. Added to what your uncle left, that should give him quite a sizeable cash flow to get things done.'

Was there no one who could remain unimpressed by Wolfe? Lindsey watched John's face as he repeated things Wolfe had said to Derek about Milk River needing every available dime poured into it. In John's eyes, it was not just sensible but admirable that Wolfe should add his own money to that which Derek considered should be hers to upgrade and improve his inheritance. That in itself, the lawyer seemed to think, was more than proof that Wolfe intended to carry on the Manston tradition at Milk River.

For a moment, Lindsey was almost swayed. Watching John's face and hearing his enthusiasm, she almost wavered. Perhaps she had been over-quick to jump to her conclusion. Perhaps if she had waited, asked—chosen a better moment, she would have got a different answer to her accusation. But no, she was forgetting. Lindsey sat bolt upright in her chair. She was forgetting Carla.

The phone had rung the day before when they had all happened to be together in the kitchen. Adeline had answered and then handed it across to Wolfe with the information that a Miss Morris was calling him. Afterwards, Wolfe had seemed more impatient with every passing minute. Now he was on his way back to the unknown Miss Morris—but could she really be in any doubt, if it came to a choice between Carla and Milk River, which one Wolfe was going to choose?

Mistaking her sudden horrified alertness for improved spirits, John beamed. 'That's better,' he said. 'There's no harm in looking on the bright side. It's natural that you should be suspicious, but given time, I think the whole situation will sort itself out.'

John stopped just as the intercom buzzer sounded on his desk and his secretary's disembodied voice echoed round the office.

'John, your wife's here.'

'Oh, lord!' John changed from a successful lawyer to a fourteen-year-old schoolboy caught in some nefarious act. 'She's expecting me to take her out to lunch, isn't she?'

'That's right!' The voice sounded faintly amused.

'And I've got to give that lecture to the Rotary Club?'

'At twelve-thirty.'

'Oh, lord!' John repeated. 'I'd forgotten Jan was coming in.' He released the intercom button and looked blankly across the desk; then his face brightened. 'Lindsey—have you got time to stop and lunch with Jan?'

'I guess so, but . . .' She was not in a lunching mood.

Once more John misunderstood. 'Nonsense, you look fine!' He took in the pants and turtleneck and the hair she had simply pulled back from her face and tied with a thin black ribbon at the nape of her neck. 'A bit pale, perhaps, but fine. A lunch'll do you good. On me, of course, and anything you want!'

'I heard that!' The door opened and Jan Miller came bustling in, her pretty little puglike face flushed from the cold outside and her carrot-top head glowing like a torch. 'I go to a lot of trouble to look my best and drive fifteen miles to lunch with the man who says he loves me, only to find out he's forgotten I exist! Come on, Lin, let's go to the Bessborough and make him pay for it!'

And that, Lindsey decided, as Jan drove them to the big Canadian National Railways hotel in the centre of downtown, that was love. Nothing, from a broken lunch date to something much more serious, was ever really likely to rock the foundations of the Millers' marriage or change the way their faces looked when they first saw each other.

They had the security of the type of love she had taken so much for granted when her uncle had been alive. She wondered if she would ever feel as secure again.

'Actually,' Jan leaned forward across the avocado and shrimp cocktails the moment they had been served, 'I've been dying to have a chat alone with you for days! What's he like?' She spooned up the first mouthful and waited with round eyes.

'What's who like?' Gossip about the Millers', children had taken them safely through Old-Fashioneds in the bar—she shouldn't drink when she was driving, but Lindsey doubted, in her present mood, that anything, far less alcohol, could have any effect—but all the time Lindsey had sensed an undercurrent of curious expectation

waiting to surface the moment they were settled
alone, at their table in the dining room, and she had
been dreading it.

'The new heir, of course!' Jan's exasperation
showed. 'And is it true that he's Marc LeBret?
Wow!' She turned round blue eyes to heaven. 'I can
remember having something of a crush on him
when he was on television a few years ago. I seem to
remember using it to make John quite jealous!' she
finished complacently.

'Then you know what he's like.' Lindsey glanced
away out of the window and watched the traffic.

'I must say that for a girl working for one of the
most intriguing-looking men I've ever seen, you
look somewhat more than a little down in the
mouth!'

Jan looked at her and Lindsey suddenly made up
her mind. If she didn't talk to someone, she'd go
mad. John understood the legal side, but could
anyone except another woman understand exactly
what was worrying her about Carla?

'Jan!' The urgent voice in her voice stopped Jan
with her spoon halfway to her mouth. 'I don't know
how much John tells you about what goes on in the
office . . . ?'

Jan shrugged. 'He talks about some things,' she
said noncommittally. 'What is it?'

'I think Wolfe might be planning to sell the
ranch!' Once started, the story came pouring out,
but this time the emphasis was different. With John
it had been finance; wills and deeds; with Jan it was
what love for Carla might make Wolfe do.

'I really wish I could help you.' Jan was still
studying her with genuine feeling in her eyes when

she dropped her off near Annabel in the downtown parking lot after a lunchtime conversation that had gone backwards and forwards across the table without reaching any positive result. 'But it's so difficult to guess what anyone in his position might have in mind. Emotions—particularly the emotion we call love—make people do strange things. One day,' she brightened, 'you'll doubtless find that out for yourself! But if you're so worried, why don't you beat this Carla person to it?'

Lindsey paused in the act of opening the door. 'What do you mean?'

'Marry him yourself! That would solve the problem. I may not be a lawyer, but I've been around John long enough to know that no one can sell a property if it belongs jointly to his wife.'

'You can't be serious!'

'No.' Jan studied her; the brilliant eyes, the hectic flush. 'No,' she went on quietly, 'of course I'm not.'

But serious or not, Lindsey could not get Jan's solution to her problems out of her head. It filled her mind. She couldn't remember how she had got out of Saskatoon, but suddenly she was passing the big potash mine and Annabel was humming along the empty highway with open prairie on either side.

It had begun to snow and she switched on the windshield wipers, willing herself to see the road and not the darkness of an angrily compelling face coming close to her; and forcing herself to feel the steering wheel and not the shock of a current like a million volts that had gripped her when their lips had touched.

Her foot slid on the accelerator and Annabel

surged ahead. Lindsey slowed down and grew more rational. How could she even think of Wolfe in terms of marriage? She was in love with Derek—she knew she was!

Besides, no matter what plans Wolfe might have for Milk River, the idea that she should marry him—even supposing he could ever want to marry her—was so preposterous as to be quite farcical. Whatever moral responsibilities she might see herself as having both to the ranch and to the people on it, no one could possibly expect her to marry to keep the estate intact.

That was something that might have been done in the first Wolfe's time—pairing off sons and daughters for the sake of land—but this was the end of the twentieth century and no one did such things.

Besides, Wolfe already had a woman in his life.

Annabel once more surged ahead, eating up the miles. Wolfe would be in Toronto with Carla before she was even home.

The first Christmas at Milk River without Ben Manston came and went. Just as Lindsey's weekly reports went in the mail to Wolfe, but there was no reply—no acknowledgement. Either he was satisfied, or he didn't care. Winter clamped down with a temperature reaching minus forty Celsius. The cattle were in the barns and in the paddocks, almost invisible behind clouds of frozen breath when they idly raised their heads to look at her whenever she went past. Work on the Pinder ranch was at a standstill now that the ground had frozen to a depth of several feet and Lindsey could look across the miles of open prairie and see nothing move except the occasional magpie flicking its long tail and screeching in the bare trees of the bush.

With nothing much to do, she wanted to do nothing; not even spend time with Derek. Now that Wolfe had barred him from the big house at Milk River, to see him she had to drive across to the farmhouse he rented. Day after day, the short daylight hours stretched emptily, but unless Derek called and insisted, it just seemed too much effort.

The first time she had seen him after her abortive trip to Saskatoon, his reaction to her suspicions about Wolfe's plans for Milk River had left her shocked and shaken.

She knew she could hardly expect him to share her devastation that everything that had been built up over generations could be going to disappear, but she had at least thought some of her obvious distress would touch him. Instead, Derek had looked at her with a glowing, jubilant face when she had broken the news.

'But that's great!' he exclaimed. 'If he does that, then he'll be the one to break the conditions of the entailment! Then, when we go to court, we won't just sue for a share of your uncle's will, we'll sue for half of everything he's got. Did you ask your lawyer about that?' he finished eagerly.

'No, I didn't.' Lindsey watched the look of eagerness disappear to be replaced by an expression of sulky irritation.

'Oh, well, I guess it doesn't matter.' Derek turned away to look out of the window at the expanse of snowbound emptiness. 'God,' he snorted, 'I can't tell you how much I want to get away from this!' He caught sight of Lindsey's face reflected in the window. 'And why not?' he demanded defensively. 'I know how much it means to you, but there's no chance that you can ever own it, is there?'

No, there wasn't. That was the one thing she had learned from her trip to Saskatoon. Wolfe owned Milk River, he could do what he liked with it, and there was nothing she could do to stop him. For the rest—whether he was actually going to sell or not— only Wolfe had the answer to that question. All she had was an accusation flung at him in anger which he had not bothered to deny and the thought of Carla always—always—there.

'Honey,' Derek tried to make things right between them, 'I know how much it all means to you, but if it's a lost cause, why shouldn't we try for everything you can get and then take off for somewhere warm? Hawaii, perhaps, or North Africa— places that'd give me what I need to write!' He pulled her to him. 'Darling, it's you I'm thinking of! With just a bit of money, we could get away. I could start work.' He gave a self-excusing little grin. 'Make you proud of me!'

For once his little-boy contrition failed to work its usual spell. Lindsey looked up at the ruffled curly hair and at the pale blue eyes gazing anxiously down at her from the handsome, slightly fleshy face and felt—nothing.

Derek was shallow and self-seeking, she suddenly realised, amazed at how unemotionally she could accept the fact, and, for the first time since he had blazed into her life, stunning her with a charm that now seemed empty and a glamour that had turned slightly false, she had her own doubts about whether he had ever had any intention of writing the novel that was going to stun the world.

He had certainly shown no signs of starting, in spite of his fine talk. The cover that had been on the typewriter when she had brought it over was not only still there but it was covered with such a thick layer of dust that she wondered if it had ever been removed. There were no paper or carbons on the table beside the window and there was certainly no manuscript; just an almost empty whisky bottle, almost ready to join the others thrown outside in the yard.

At least in one thing Wolfe had been absolutely right, she had to grant him that. Derek was no writer. He was probably even no more than a second-rate actor, if the truth were known, otherwise he would have stayed where the work was in Toronto, not buried himself in this out-of-the-way place.

How lucky he must have thought himself when he discovered that he had chosen one of the few places in the country where the local landowner's niece was so impressionable and naïve that she could be swept off her feet by the impact of his apparent glamour and worldly charm—and what a shock it must have been when he discovered that his infatuated heiress was not an heiress after all.

She supposed the hurt that he had just been using her would come later, but for the moment, it was almost a relief to be able to see through his flashy, superficial charm, and she wondered how she could ever have thought she had been in love.

She took his arms from around her waist and put them to his side. 'Derek, I've got to go.'

'But I'll see you tomorrow, won't I?' For the first time ever, Derek was asking *her* for reassurance: not questioning her decision but scanning her face anxiously, quite unlike his usual sulky self whenever he was thwarted.

Lindsey remembered the countless times when she had been in the position of trying to change his mood. 'I don't know about tomorrow,' she said quietly. 'I've got a lot of work to do.'

He neither pressed her nor tried to make her change her mind. Instead, he followed her outside to the farm truck she had brought across, and he was still standing in the unkempt yard in the biting wind when she glanced into the rear view mirror as she turned out of the drive. His jeans and his brightly coloured, open-necked silk shirt made him look flamboyant, but at the same time he was pathetic. Like a man marooned on a desert island watching the last ship sail away.

Lindsey still had not raised the question of his unpaid rent, she suddenly realised, and that she would have to do if she was not to face another episode of Wolfe's stinging contempt. But—she took her foot off the brake pedal and went on—it would do another day.

'But why?' Lindsey followed the young man and his clipboard from fireplace to the table beside the front door and watched him write. 'Why is it necessary to have an inventory? The surveyor was here a week ago and he seemed satisfied.' At least, he had left her with a copy of his list of the major repairs he said were necessary on the house and she had forwarded it to Wolfe. And now this other man had appeared, arranged for, like the surveyor, by Wolfe himself but without a word to her. He had just arrived at the back door earlier, declaring that he had been sent to do an inventory of the contents and producing a letter with Wolfe's signature and a card which indentified him as belonging to a major firm of auctioneers and valuers.

He and his clipboard had taken over, and Lindsey had at first stood stunned and then followed him almost automatically as he had gone from room to room, crushed by the casual way in which he appraised and then listed objects she had loved and lived with all her life.

'Why?' Standing in the draught that always came whistling under the front door whenever the wind was in the north, the valuer—young, in his mid-twenties with bright red hair—went on writing and did not look up. 'It's fairly routine for someone who's inherited an old place like this to have a content valuation made. If it's not been done for donkey's years, who knows what you might find. A long-lost masterpiece, perhaps! Though,' he looked up from his clipboard long enough to glance around the hall, 'I wouldn't say there's much chance of that today!'

'But why?' Lindsey persisted. 'I still don't understand?'

'Why have a valuation?' The young man shrugged. 'I dunno. It depends what the owner has in mind. Sale, perhaps, or insurance—it's up to him. He's the one who's paying the bill. Say, this isn't bad!'

Sale, perhaps, or insurance. Lindsey was still absorbing it with a sickening sense of knowing which one it was when the young man pushed aside the books and papers covering the top of the table beside the door. Her uncle had always kept his farm journals on that table, piling them up in stacks and furious if they were disturbed.

'It's early Colonial, I think. American New England pine. It's criminal to keep it here when you think what it's worth!' He was laughing as he glanced up, but at the sight of Lindsey's face, his laughter died. 'I'm sorry,' he said, 'that wasn't very tactful, was it? In a job like this, you sometimes forget it's not just price but sentimental value.' Slightly ashamed, he started to turn away, but then looked back, as if really seeing Lindsey for the first time. 'Say,' his face brightened, 'would you have dinner with me tonight?'

Lindsey refused. This sudden and obvious admiration had only, paradoxically, made her feel more depressed. If she was so eye-catching and attractive, what was she doing here, standing helplessly on one side as the first steps were being taken to destroy her home?

No, not her home—Lindsey dug her fingers into her palms until her nails left deep white marks. It was Wolfe's home. His, and if he wanted, Carla's! He had every right to have an inventory made: for insurance—or for sale.

In that moment she had never felt more isolated and alone, and it was a feeling even Jan couldn't alter when she called later that day.

'Hi! What have you been up to? I thought we would have seen you over Christmas or New Year!' Jan sounded bright and happy.

Lindsey shrugged. 'I've been busy.' Doing nothing, as the old song said.

'Okay, then, all the more reason for you to accept!'

'Accept what?'

'An invitation. John's just about established his practice now, so I thought entertaining a few of his more important clients wouldn't come amiss plus, to liven things up a bit, some of our friends as well. 'You,' Jan paused and then rushed quickly on, 'and Wolfe. D'you think he'd come?'

'Why not? He's in Toronto, but you could ask him.' Lindsey hoped she sounded less wooden than she felt. 'Hang on and I'll get you his address.' And phone number, she added privately. If Carla answered, let her decide if she was going to let Wolfe accept or not. Except, even as she thought it, Lindsey knew that she was wrong. No one decided for Wolfe Manston except the man himself.

Seconds later, Jan was repeating the seven numbers to make sure she had got them right. 'I'll get the area code number from the book,' she said happily. 'It's probably ridiculous, thinking he'll come all this way, but you never know.'

No, you didn't, Lindsey thought. Just as you didn't know what he really thought of you or of the inheritance which was his to sell or keep.

'Wait a moment, I haven't given you the date.' Jan stopped her on the run up to goodbye. 'I thought the twenty-fifth. January's such a dead month—a party should cheer everybody up!'

This time goodbyes were said and Lindsey replaced the telephone. Nothing, absolutely nothing, could cheer her up.

CHAPTER SEVEN

LINDSEY was in the four-wheel-drive farm truck, not riding Fire Bird, and ground that had been brown and dead in the fall was hard and white and covered with winter snow, but otherwise, everything was just the same as it had been on that first day.

Lindsey crested the swale above the frozen slough behind the house and stopped. A car was in the drive out front—a car that had most certainly not been there when she had left to drive across to the Pinders' place. Long, sleek and white, it stood out clearly against the dark background of the fir trees in the windbreak. Wolfe had come. She had never expected it, but he had. He had flown back for Jan's party and, maybe, for something else.

She shifted her booted foot from brake to gas pedal. Sitting here wondering would do no good. Wolfe was here and she had to face him, and if he had used the excuse of Jan's party to come back and break the news that Milk River was going to be sold, she would have to face that, too.

The truck bounced over the rutted snow as she headed down towards the slough and the white car disappeared behind the house. Once more, it was remarkable how everything still looked the same, but it was six months now since Ben Manston's death and nothing, any more, could ever be the same.

'He's here!' Adeline wore a look of suppressed excitement on her brown face as Lindsey opened the kitchen door. 'The new boss is here!'

At least it was still 'the new boss'. With all his charm and power—over everyone except her, Lindsey grimly told herself—Wolfe hadn't quite managed to blot out Ben's memory from Milk River.

'And he's brought someone with him.' Adeline got Lindsey's attention back. 'A Miss Morris, I think he said her name was, and it seems she's staying on. At least, he's had me get one of the rooms in the front ready for her.' Adeline went rattling on, too bound up in the excitement of the moment to notice Lindsey's face. '. . . they're in the hall now, having coffee, and he said for you to go straight through directly you came in.' Now she noticed. At least, she noticed the set white face; no one could know about the feeling of having suddenly been turned to stone with all reactions dead and feelings numb. 'There's nothing wrong, is there?' Adeline queried.

'No, nothing.' Lindsey mechanically closed the inner door behind the outer storm door. Of course there was nothing wrong! Not unless you counted the fact that Adeline's news had made her even colder than she already was; colder even than the draught of freezing air she had brought in with her to the kitchen. Carla Morris had arrived, that was all; the woman with whom Wolfe shared his life.

She refused to think why the fact affected her so much, preferring instead to concentrate on other things. Such as why Wolfe had brought Carla with him, for example. Was it just to have a partner for

Jan's party, or was it so that Carla could confirm what she, Lindsey, already half suspected? That Wolfe would be crazy to take on the responsibilities of Milk River when he could so easily sell it.

'The new boss said for you to go straight through when you came in.' Adeline's prompting cut through her train of thought.

'What? Oh, yes.' Lindsey glanced down at the jeans and boots and the quilted vest and sheepskin coat in which she seemed to live. She suddenly and desperately longed to go and change—to compete with the immaculately groomed and elegant woman she imagined Carla to be. But that was quite ridiculous. Not only did she have no time to change, she had no reason to compete. She pulled off her sheepskin jacket and tossed it on the nearest chair together with her hat and gloves. 'I'll go through straight away.'

The quiet closing of the swing door underneath the stairs did not disturb the conversation going on between the two people sitting on the couch in front of the blazing fire. A small wheeled trolley bearing coffee cups and, Lindsey noticed, the silver service, had been pushed slightly to one side, and although the lights had not been switched on, the man's profile, at least, was easy enough to recognise against its background of leaping flames.

Lindsey's heart also leaped as she absorbed it along with an earlier memory, not of a profile but of a face with fine-grained olive skin beneath dark hair and grey eyes glowing as the mouth came ever closer down towards hers.

So Wolfe had kissed her. She jerked her mind back to the present from that kiss. It meant nothing—nothing!—just as Wolfe meant nothing to her. If it had not been for the accident of birth and heritage, he would never have come into her life.

The woman sitting next to him was more difficult to see. She was leaning back against the couch in an easy, relaxed way with the smoke from her cigarette forming a graceful plume above her head. As Lindsey watched, she laughed—a deep, throaty laugh—and leaned forward and rested her hand on Wolfe's arm.

She was talking about Milk River and the voice was the one Lindsey had heard coming down the telephone, but it was the casual intimacy of the gesture that made a hard, small knot form in the base of Lindsey's throat, and the pain of her reaction had nothing to do with the future of Milk River and everything to do with Wolfe.

Something—Lindsey's indrawn breath, maybe, or just the sense of someone standing there—drew Wolfe's attention to the shadows underneath the stairs.

'Lindsey?' He got up and walked towards her, questioning at first but then with a smile that set her nerve ends tingling. The mouth now curved and smiling was the one that she had kissed; the hand now reaching out for hers had once rested on her spine, drawing her close to the hard contours of the body beneath that elegantly tailored charcoal worsted suit.

Lindsey fought against unbidden memory and lost.

'You're cold.' He took her hand and his thumb brushed against her wrist.

She couldn't think; couldn't hear what else he said. All she could do was feel the pressure of his fingers and watch the movement of his lips.

'Yes, I've been out.' For a moment, there were just two people in the hall. Herself and Wolfe.

'Darling, don't keep her standing there. I'm longing to meet her. Bring her here!'

Darling! Lindsey snatched her hand away, but why was she so upset? Of course Carla would call Wolfe darling, she had guessed it for three months. What was so upsetting about something she had already guessed?

'Lindsey Kinsale—Carla Morris.' Lindsey had walked rigidly erect towards the figure on the couch and she could hear the sardonic glint in Wolfe's eyes as he introduced them.

'How do you do?' Lindsey held out a hand—the hand still warm from the pressure of Wolfe's fingers.

Carla didn't move but went on sitting with her small, elegantly shingled head against the back of the couch and her eyes half closed against the smoke rising from her cigarette. Like the long jade holder, the eyes were green and the hair was blonde, almost white blonde, not like Lindsey's duller gold. It clung to the finely sculptured head and showed the regular small features of the face to perfection.

All in all, the Carla of flesh and blood was exactly as Lindsey had imagined on the telephone. Striking in a black travelling suit and high-heeled boots; sophisticated, utterly composed and also, very clearly, bored.

'How do you do?' She did not take Lindsey's

hand but leaned forward to crush out her barely
smoked cigarette. When she did look up, however,
a slight amusement seemed to have replaced her
earlier bored indifference.

Faded jeans, an elderly quilted vest over a
turtlenecked sweater in an unbecoming shade of
almond green and a face, flushed scarlet now, no
doubt, under the pale sweep of severely drawn
back hair. Lindsey saw herself through Carla's eyes
and felt like a grubby child summoned from the
yard to meet an unexpected visitor.

If Carla had ever thought in terms of competition, there was obviously no competition now.

'So this is Lindsey, is it?' Green eyes flicked past
her. 'Why didn't you tell me, Wolfe? She looks
such a babe to have so much responsibility!'

'Carla!' Lindsey sensed Wolfe move behind her.
'If you'll stop being such a bitch, my love, I can
explain to Lindsey why we're here.'

It was said equably, without malice, but the
authority was there. Carla, however, merely smiled
and leaned forward for another cigarette.

Wolfe had come to her defence, but Lindsey felt
even worse. The incident had only underlined his
closeness with the woman on the couch. What
chance was there for Milk River in that relationship? What chance was there for her? She
turned abruptly, brushing against Wolfe's jacket
with her sleeve. It was cloth against cloth, but
even so, the tension sparked and shot along her
arm.

'Jan Miller called about her party.' Wolfe did not
appear to notice her quickly lowered eyes. 'But you
know that, I think?'

'Yes.' Lindsey stayed watching the knot of a dark silk tie.

'It seemed a good reason to come back.' The French-edged voice above her head went on. 'My book about Australia's finished—or at least, at the proof reading stage, and I don't have to be in Toronto to do that.' She heard him smile; imagined the direction of his look. 'I thought the break would do us good.'

Us. Wolfe and Carla! Us!

'We'll be staying for a night or two—perhaps longer. It depends what Carla wants to do.'

He stayed smiling at a silent but watchful Carla, and this time, Lindsey understood. Obviously whether they stayed or not *would* depend on what Carla wanted to do. So much for Wolfe's talk about the continuity of Milk River and his sense of belonging there, if Carla only had to crook her little finger to have him leave.

At least, though, they were observing the proprieties. While they were here, they were sleeping in separate rooms. Spending the night together would mean a midnight walk around the landing running around the upper level of the hall. No wonder Carla was looking so bored and indifferent. If it was left to Carla, they would be on the next flight back to Toronto and the apartment that was home.

In that moment, Lindsey had no doubt that Wolfe planned to sell the ranch.

'I see.' Her voice was tight and hard. They looked so right together—Wolfe dark and carrying his own special power; Carla blonde and almost fragile on the over-padded couch. The only thing not fragile was the expression on Carla's face, shrewd and enigmatic, looking first at Lindsey and then at Wolfe. Wolfe might not guess, but Carla knew exactly what thoughts were running through Lindsey's wildly spinning head.

'Excuse me.' Suddenly she could bear it all no longer; the intimacy, the secrets that they clearly shared. 'Excuse me, but I have some work to do.'

'Leave it!'

Wolfe stopped her, but she persisted. 'I'm afraid I can't.'

'Why not?' His face was quizzical, amused, and her heart turned over. 'It'll still be there tomorrow. Why don't you go and change,' he looked at her old clothes, 'and then we'll all go out to dinner and go straight on to Jan's.'

He thought it was so easy, pulling wool over her eyes, but for all that Carla thought, she was not a child and the equivalent of candy could not appease her.

'I'm afraid I can't.' Was it really her, answering in the same nasal, offhand tone of voice that Carla had? 'I've already made arrangements to go with someone else tonight.' It was a double lie. She was not going to Jan's party and she was most certainly not going with anyone. But they pitied her—Wolfe with his smile and Carla with her curious sideways glance—and she would prove that no one had to pity her. Milk River might be sold around her ears and Derek had already proved that he cared more about her money than he cared for her, but the last thing she planned to be was pitiable.

'Oh?' Wolfe's eyebrows rose and the question hung between them.

'Yes.' Lindsey rushed on, not stopping to consider the consequences of turning query into outright challenge. 'I'm going with Derek Foster—I'm sure you remember him?'

'Yes, I do.' A white line formed around Wolfe's mouth. 'I had also hoped that you would have had the sense to see through that charlatan by now.' Across the intervening space, his eyes were no longer grey but black chips of slate. 'I realise I was wrong.'

His derision stung and hurt, but before she could reply, he had moved away to stand with one arm resting on the mantleshelf, gazing down into the fire, leaving her with only Carla's clear amusement at the interchange for company.

She had said she had more work to do—another lie—but suddenly all that mattered was that she should get away. Lindsey turned and almost ran for the stairs and the refuge of her room. When she was halfway up, Wolfe might have called after her, but she did not stop, and it was Carla's light contralto laugh that came floating in as she slammed her bedroom door.

She stood there, leaning back with her hands outstretched against the door's comforting solidity. Why had she done—said—what she had? But whatever demon had possessed her, there was now no backing down. After hearing Carla's laugh, she just had to do what she had said, and that—the thought sobered her—meant driving across to the old Kersey place and asking Derek if he would go with her to Jan's party.

'Lindsey!'

Her stomach jack-knifed and Lindsey stopped. She had thought she was going to be able to leave and go to Derek's with no one seeing her. That was why she had listened when she had opened her bedroom door and then crept down the back stairs to the kitchen—a thief in her own home—to get the sheepskin jacket she had left lying on the chair. Wolfe and Carla would still be where she had left them, laughing about her in the hall, but even Jake or Adeline were suddenly too much to face, and that was why she had made sure the coast was clear and the kitchen empty before she had come creeping down.

But now, however, Wolfe was there, behind her, standing in the open doorway leading to the hall. With all the light on her and none on him, he looked like a black statue made of hard unpolished stone.

She turned reluctantly. 'Yes? What do you want?'

'What I want is to shake some sense into your head. What I'll settle for is asking if you realise what a fool you're making of yourself!'

'I don't know what you mean.' Lindsey was defiant.

'Really?' He stepped into the light and Lindsey tensed. 'Then let me tell you. We share a name—the Manston name. It may not be yours,' he stopped her quick protest, 'but it's part of the bloodline and heritage we share and I have no intention of allowing it to be made a local laughing stock. Foster's a fool, Lindsey, a self-serving idiot.' His intensity frightened her. 'You know that as well as I do, but you're choosing to be blind. Tell me—' he stopped her as she tried to turn away with his finger and thumb on either side of her jaw and his palm against her throat, 'what does it take to get you to understand that Foster's using you?'

For a second, she just stood there; mesmerised by his look, his voice, his touch. Watching his lips but imagining them take the place of his hand against her throat, brushing down towards the pulse spot leaping wildly at its base. She felt weightless, hollow, totally bereft of will; pliant as his fingers tightened underneath her jaw—but then their bodies brushed and she sprang away.

Reality was a longing he would never satisfy. Reality was Carla laughing in the hall.

'In that case, you and Derek have a lot in common.' For once, she took him by surprise.

Slate eyes narrowed and the mouth that had been above hers snapped into a hard, straight line. 'And what exactly do you mean by that?' he grated out.

'Well, aren't you also using me?' It was her turn to drawl. 'I'm convenient, that's why I'm here. If it wasn't for me, you wouldn't be able to go off to Toronto and—' she paused and thought of Carla, but she wasn't brave enough, '—and write your books. I hardly think you can accuse Derek of something that you do yourself! And now, if you'll excuse me,' she bent and picked up her coat, 'I've an errand I have to run.'

Wolfe neither contradicted nor tried to stop her, but stood and watched her as she struggled with her heavy coat. He was still standing, motionless, as she went out through the door.

Not that she expected—or wanted—him to con-
tradict her or explain; not that she cared. Three of
the six months of his farce of a contract binding her
to stay on at Milk River had expired. The situation
was quite intolerable, and she was leaving—soon.
Let him whistle for his ranch manager for the next
three months; let him console himself with Carla or
let him sell. Either way, she would not be there to
see.

She got into Annabel and roared out of the yard,
throwing the old car at the turning into the side
road leading to the old Kersey place. She needed
speed to blot the picture of Wolfe and Carla from
her mind, and the road stopped at Derek's farmhouse: no one was likely to be driving the other
way.

She saw it as she straightened; the same old black
Buick, built like a tank, that had screeched off from
the farmhouse when she had been there with Wolfe
what now seemed an eternity ago. It was speeding
down the narrow road towards her with what
seemed like inches between it and the snow-filled
ditch on either side. It came on without slowing,
but, in the way fear had of turning everything into
the slow motion of unreality, she had more than
time to recognise the driver behind the wheel. It
was the same man. A big, powerful-looking brute;
no one she knew; no one who lived locally. She
could even see the broken boxer's nose between
the close-set eyes as he sounded his horn viciously
and forced her to give way.

Somehow they passed; somehow the car shot
away, slewing and slithering on the drifting snow as
it took the turn and disappeared in the direction of

the highway leading to Saskatoon. Lindsey slowed down and drove on, but she was still alarmed.

What had the car been doing there? If it had been the first time she had seen it, she might have assumed that the driver had lost his way and taken the turn to the old Kersey place by mistake, but this was the second time he had been there and he would hardly make the same mistake twice. He looked so unlike Derek's description of his friends from his Toronto theatre days, and yet he must have been coming from the cottage.

Even though she was no longer blinded by infatuation, Lindsey was still concerned. At the very least, Derek's visitor was a careless brute. The way he had been driving, he could have killed them both! Lindsey shivered as she parked Annabel and followed in the tracks of a much large set of footprints through the snow to the farmhouse door.

She knocked. 'Derek!' She knocked again and this time she called. There had been no reply to her first knock, but she sensed that he was there.

'Derek!' Thoroughly alarmed by now, she rattled the latch, but the door was bolted from the inside, something it had never been in the past when she had called. 'Derek—it's me!' she tried again. 'Lindsey!'

This time there were footsteps; just a few, as if Derek had been standing against the wall between the window and the door where he could not be seen. Then she heard the bolt go back and he was there—and at first sight, she barely recognised him.

Standing in the doorway with the brilliant light reflected from the snow bouncing straight onto

him, he seemed smaller, somehow, and shrunken
and scared with a pinched white face from which
the usual self-assurance had been drained away. A
mark that could have been the beginnings of a
bruise showed faintly on his cheekbone and the
heavy silver medallion he always wore around his
neck was missing, leaving his throat bare and
curiously vulnerable with an angry red weal on the
pallid skin as if someone had caught hold of the
medallion and wrenched it off.

Lindsey noticed all this as the door opened, and
yet none of it really registered. What did reach out
and grip her was Derek's obvious fear.

'Derek—what's wrong?'

'Come in.' Instead of answering, he grabbed
her wrist and pulled her inside, then he shut and
bolted the door. 'God,' he muttered, 'I need a
drink!'

He went across to the table beside an overturned
chair and poured himself a whisky, bottle clattering
against the rim of the smeared glass. He gulped the
neat drink back and poured another.

'Derek!' By now thoroughly alarmed, Lindsey's
voice rose. 'You must tell me! What's wrong?
What's been happening?'

'Wrong? Nothing's wrong.' he replied belligerently, but the look he gave her was almost
furtive and there was a nasal, backstreets twang in
his voice that she had never heard before.

But yes, she had. It had been there that day at the
house when she had found him waiting for her. The
day she had first seen the black car racing from the
farmhouse. In the ensuing argument with Wolfe,
she had forgotten, but just for a few seconds,

Derek's rounded Upper Canada College accent had been missing, just as it was missing now.

'Why should there be anything wrong?' Derek's confidence was returning as the drink took hold and so was his normal voice.

Lindsey pushed the riddle to one side; she had other things to worry her. 'I passed a car in the lane just now and it almost had me in the ditch—and now you, here, like this!' She nodded at the overturned chair and at papers strewn all over the floor. There had been a fight, she realised, and Derek had come off second best.

'What car?' He did his best to look puzzled.

'Derek, don't lie to me! I know it must have been here. The road stops here, so where else could it have been? Besides,' she paused, 'I've seen it here before.'

'Oh!' He stopped trying to pretend. 'That was a friend—someone from the old days. I owed him some money and he got a bit excited, that's all. But it's settled now—it's fine!' He took another mouthful of neat whisky, halving the level in the glass and watching her across the rim.

'Are you sure?' He was holding something back, she knew it.

'Oh, for God's sake, Lin, let it drop!' The alcohol had given his blue eyes an angry glitter and he looked quite menacing. 'Anyway, what's brought you here?' he asked abruptly. 'What do you want?'

Lindsey gave up. Derek was entitled to his secrets—and besides, she had to tell him why she was here even though, seeing him standing there, pathetic and somehow hollow with all his courage

coming from the half empty glass, she wondered
how she could ever have thought she loved him and
knew that he was the last person with whom she
wanted to go to the Millers' party that night.

But she had to. She had flung down the gauntlet
at the sight of Wolfe and Carla both in league
against her and she could not back down now. 'I've
been invited to a party at the Millers'—you know,
Derek had met them once. 'John and Jan, in
Saskatoon. I wondered if you'd come with me. It's
tonight.'

'I see!' Derek's lips twisted. 'Having avoided me
for weeks, you've now decided that I'm good
enough for all your smart friends to see me with
you, have you? What's the matter, Cinderella? Has
Prince Charming turned you down?'

It hurt, it hurt more than it should, but Lindsey
did not react. There was some justification in
what he said. 'Derek, don't let's fight. We both
know that everything's over between us, don't
we?—but is there any reason why we can't be
friends?'

He looked at her with a completely new expression of respect. 'You really have grown up all of a
sudden, haven't you?' he said quietly, then he
gulped down the remaining whisky and banged the
glass down on the table. 'Okay,' he said, 'I'll come.
What time?'

'I'll pick you up about seven. We can have a
coffee and a sandwich somewhere on the way.' Jan
was having a buffet supper, but it was a two-hour
drive to Saskatoon. If they got there late, they
could eat and leave and she would have to spend no
more than an hour or two watching Wolfe with

Carla and keeping up a pretence of happiness. 'Oh, and Derek,' she looked up at him. 'Wolfe will be there.'

CHAPTER EIGHT

IT was probably the worst evening of Lindsey's life. No—that had been when Ben had died, but this was just as awful, though in a different way.

Derek was drunk. He had been slightly drunk when she had picked him up shortly after seven and he had insisted on stopping at a hotel and not a diner on the way. By the time Jan's buffet was announced, food was past saving him, and Lindsey could hear his over-loud talk and laughter as he went from group to group, easy to pick out in a satin shift open to the waist and tightly fitting leather pants and pointed boots—the evening's urban cowboy.

'I must say you know some extraordinary men!' Jan came up to Lindsey standing on the sidelines, saw her empty hands and glanced towards the buffet table. 'Aren't you going to eat?'

'No. No, thanks,' Lindsey said miserably. 'I'm sorry,' she meant Derek. 'I'm really sorry, Jan.'

'No need.' Jan was practical. 'It's not your fault, and besides, one more than compensates for the other. I'm going to get the reputation of the hostess with the mostest if I go on like this. Did you see them all when Wolfe came in? They couldn't believe their eyes. They come to a little old party in little old Saskatoon and they get to meet an author who's known halfway round the world. And you're the person who got him here!' Jan said emphatically. 'He wouldn't have come if it hadn't been for you.' Not true, Lindsey thought, but comforting. 'So don't worry, hon. As I said, one of your men more than compensates for the other!'

Lindsey looked down at the silk folds of her dress. One of her men! Wolfe had barely glanced at her all evening. 'It's kind of you, but I still feel terrible!' At least that was true.

'Well, don't.' Jan's eyes went to the largest group around the buffet table; a group surrounding one dark head. She couldn't leave the subject of Wolfe alone. 'But did you *see* them when he came in?' she said happily. 'I thought he was going to get eaten up. No wonder that Carla person of his won't take her hands off him!'

Yes, Lindsey had seen Wolfe when he had come in, and she had seen the way Carla's scarlet nails stayed dug into the dark cloth of his jacket. Automatically, instinctively, along with everybody else, her eyes had been drawn to the doorway of the big open-plan living room, and she had watched with a dry mouth and rapidly pumping heart as Wolfe had stood there on the threshold with Carla clinging to his arm.

For a moment, there had been no one between them and Wolfe had looked at her; dismissive, contemptuous, all that and more had been written in the curved flare of his nostrils and the hard lines of his face as he had glanced from her to Derek and then back again. It had taken just a moment, and then he had been almost mobbed.

Until that second, Lindsey had had no idea how well known he was. His head and Carla's blonde one had almost disappeared as, at first diffident and then competing, both men and women had jockeyed to be introduced and then stayed to talk and listen to the internationally known Marc LeBret.

His dual identity just added to the glamorous aura surrounding him. Wolfe Manston—Marc LeBret, she could hear the names being mentioned even now as two women sat nearby and ate their buffet supper and went on talking.

For once, Wolfe had no need of the special quality of charm and power that had such an impact on everyone he met. A series he had hosted had apparently just finished its run on the Public Broadcasting Service piped in to Saskatoon from North Dakota on cable television. It had made his face immediately recognisable to anyone with the slightest interest in books and authors—and that certainly meant this affluent, middle-class crowd—but, far from cable television, Milk River did not even get good reception from the nearest ordinary transmitter and Lindsey had long ago given up on the snowstorm of black and white that greeted her whenever she switched on her set.

So much for living in the boondocks, she thought ironically. She must have been the one person in the crowded room totally unaware of just how famous the man whose whereabouts her consciousness could pinpoint every second really was.

'Are you sure I can't get you anything?' Jan once more nodded at her empty hands.

'No—no, thanks. I'm not really hungry,' Lindsey half apologised. Jan had gone to so much trouble. Everything, from ham and turkey and salmon de-

corated in aspic to Ukrainian pyroshkies with dill
and sour cream dressing, was on the buffet table.
'Maybe I'll go and get something later when there
aren't so many people.'

They both heard Derek's raucous laugh.

'I should try and force something into him, as
well,' said Jan. 'If it's not too late!' she added.
'Anyway, if you're sure you're okay here, I'd better
go and mingle.'

'Yes, do.' Lindsey watched Jan move across the
room, stopping here and talking there but always,
without any real deviation, heading towards the
group surrounding Wolfe.

There was another laugh. Not, this time, Derek
but a man standing in Wolfe's group. It didn't seem
to matter, Lindsey thought. Man or woman, they
both fell under the spell Wolfe's own special quality. She watched him covertly through half-closed
lashes—smile glinting, head slightly on one side, a
face alive with interest as he listened to what was
being said and then, in his turn, laughed with a
quiet chuckle and that still came clearly across the
room.

The pattern of the crowd changed and Lindsey
lost him. Marc LeBret, best-selling author and
now, as she had discovered, a household name and
face on television. Was it really likely that he would
ever want to be just plain Wolfe Manston and turn
his back on everything to keep Milk River? Certainly not if Carla, whose silvery blonde head close
to his had just become visible through the intervening people, had any say in his decision.

'Snobbish bunch, your friends, aren't they?' De-
feated by half-turned backs and a series of polite

unspoken refusals to include him in any conversation, Derek sought her out as she stood, half obscured by the green folds of the curtains which she had hoped would offer protective cover for the green silk of her dress.

Someone somewhere had put on the stereo and dancing was starting to begin on the glassed-in patio with its view of stars above and the frozen North Saskatchewan river and the city lights below.

'It's probably because they don't know you.' She should suggest that he had had enough to drink and take the half-full wine glass from his hand. But a scene was near the surface, and she couldn't bear a scene.

'That doesn't seem to bother our Lord of the Manor!' Derek's voice was jealous and his eyes held a spiteful glitter.

Lindsey looked at the flushed and discontented face. Had she ever really been so naïve—Wolfe's word: she winced—as to think she was in love with this flashy, embittered man?

'Perhaps we should go home?' She tried it carefully.

Derek emptied his glass in an almost aggressive fashion. 'Not on your life! I'm going to get through to this bunch of stuffed shirts if it takes me all night!' He noticed her empty hands. 'Do you want a drink?'

'No, and don't you think . . . ?'

'In that case, you won't mind if I drink your share for you!' Derek wove his way across the room to the impromptu bar.

She should go with him. He was her partner, her

responsibility—but she stayed exactly where she was as the music appeared to get louder and more people joined the dancers on the patio.

She couldn't see them, but Wolfe and Carla must be dancing—at least, they were no longer near the buffet. She could see Derek, though, turning in her direction and looking as if the room was slightly out of focus. Lindsay drew back behind the curtains.

What a way to spend an evening! Hiding from your partner and looking for the man you loved.

The thought brought her sharply upright. What on earth had put that idea into her head? She wasn't in love with Wolfe—but she was. Her mind and body told her; nerves fluttering and full of tension as they got the message to remember being held against him while his mouth came slowly down on hers. She remembered everything about it, and her lips remembered. Standing there, she ran her tongue across them, feeling the once unbearably sensitive flesh and the even more sensitive response of a movement that had made them part beneath his passionate exploration.

Her whole body curved, reliving the brush of his as he bent her to him, crushing her breasts and moulding her thighs to his. That had been the moment she had loved him, wanting more than he would offer or she could have. That had been the moment she had sprung from him and hurled the accusation that he planned to sell Milk River at his head.

Fingers that had been buried in his hair abruptly clenched and the smooth silk of her dress was like a rasp against skin that was suddenly unbearably sensitive.

Dancers whirled on the lighted patio, but she no longer saw.

She had loved Wolfe for three months and denied it. No—she had loved him for even longer. The kiss she was remembering had sprung from his contemptuous allegation that Derek was a charlatan, but maybe she had loved him since the day she had walked into the farm office and seen a man so strong, so sure, so powerful and totally unexpected that, from that moment on, Derek's sham lustre had begun to lose its brilliance.

She shuddered and let out her breath, and the present came rushing back to overwhelm her; standing on the sidelines, an outsider at Jan's party. If there had ever been a chance of meaning anything to Wolfe, it was gone as surely as the future of Milk River.

She had defied and fought him; done anything to deny a knowledge that had, all the time, been slowly growing, and now here she was, watching him dancing on the patio with Carla in his arms.

Carla! She at least was some bitter consolation. Even if she had acknowledged her secret feelings, Carla had already been there, part of Wolfe's life— his Marc LeBret life—which had never held a place for her or Milk River.

The pattern of dancers changed and Carla and Wolfe were straight in front of her, framed in the open doorway to the patio like a picture.

The chiffon of Carla's dress was drifting around Wolfe's legs—their bodies must be touching—and

his whole stance was protective as he looked down
and listened to what she had to say. They turned,
one easy fluid movement to the music, two people
joined as one, and as Wolfe raised his head above
Carla's bare shoulder, his eyes caught Lindsey's
and the laughter in his face went out.

'Come on, Lindsey Kinsale! It's about time you
stopped hiding behind drapes and started dancing!'
Another face, pink and smiling, interposed itself
between her and Wolfe.

She must have known its owner—at least, he
spoke as if she did—unless he had been dragooned
by Jan into rescuing her from her corner, but
Lindsey never really saw him. She went obediently
to the floor and fitted herself into a pair of arms.
She danced, she talked, maybe she smiled—she
even heard a slight commotion from the direction
of the buffet in the other room—but all the time
deep purple eyes were clouded with the memory of
the expression on Wolfe's face.

Hard, dismissive, biting, he had held her with a
look that seared right through her, and, on the edge
of her field of vision, his hand had rested on Carla's
naked back.

She had learned everything about jealousy in
that moment. The scalding pain that had consumed
her made every other emotion she had ever felt
seem commonplace: her infatuation for Derek no
more than the teenage crush she should have had at
seventeen as part of the experience of growing up.
Maybe it took jealousy—writhing, snarling
jealousy, before you were mature.

The music stopped but almost immediately re-
started, and the owner of the pink and smiling

face went to draw her to him.

'No!' Lindsey shook her head. Think of an excuse; any excuse. 'I'm sorry. I enjoyed it, but I've . . . I've got rather a headache.'

Wolfe was too close, just two couples from them. She had to get away, find Derek and persuade him to go home.

In her haste, she over-trod the heel of her high, strappy sandals and her ankle twisted painfully. She reached out and clutched the nearest arm to save herself.

'I'm sorry!' The woman whose arm she clutched looked down startled and Lindsey apologised. The doorway was ahead of her. She chose her moment and tried to get through the closely packed dancers.

'I'm sorry!' She apologised for the third and fourth times as she brushed against them, but the door was close now, just two yards away. She had almost reached it when fingers gripped her elbow and turned her back into the crowded room.

'Have you any idea what a fool you're making of yourself?' An arm went round her waist and another face, not pink and smiling or female and selfconscious but hard and cold with granite chips for eyes, was in front of her. 'This appears to be a waltz,' said Wolfe, 'so dance it!'

If she thought just of his arm, strong and secure against her waist, leading her and turning her to avoid the other couples, it might have been possible to forget about the scathing coldness in his voice; ignore the fact of Carla and the fact of the dispersal of Milk River and concentrate on nothing except being close to him. She could feel the warmth of him against her; warmth overlaying muscle and the inner core of will.

'When this dance is over.' Wolfe was talking to a spoiled and fractious child. 'You'll find Jan and thank her and then you'll leave—with us!'

'It strikes me there are two things wrong with that!' Lindsey was pleased with her reaction. No one could guess that her skin was melting where they touched. She pushed providence even further, tilting her head under its specially piled up crown of hair the colour of winter wheat to look up at him. She could see herself, two tiny images in a field of grey shading from only slightly darker pupils, her own eyes wide, her chin firm and determined. 'Firstly, I'm not ready to leave just yet, and secondly, I came with Derek and I'm going home with him!' She made home sound like more than home, and his fingers almost broke her wrist.

'In that case, you've got a problem!' He was cynical and amused in a dead set face.

'Why? What do you mean?' Providence had failed her; she had overstepped the mark.

'If you were planning to sleep with Foster, then you're too late!' Wolfe snapped. 'Foster's upstairs already, dead to the world. He started some sort of argument at the bar and then passed out. Jan and John have agreed to keep him until the morning.'

Lindsey was absolutely crushed. 'Oh, I see.' Her small voice filled the silence as the music stopped.

'So,' Wolfe was openly contemptuous, 'Do I say good night and leave you here, or do we both go and find Jan and say goodbye?'

'But we—I—' Lindsey focussed on his mouth; at least that way she could keep the top of her head to him, 'I came in Annabel.'

'Leave the keys, and Foster,' the mouth twisted, 'can drive your car back in the morning when he's recovered.'

'And I go home with you and Carla?' She raised her face to a guarded, hard expression.

'Yes,' said Wolfe.

Carla! Carla! Carla! For the next few days, everything was geared to Carla. What she wanted and what she thought. It started on the drive back from Saskatoon. Lindsey sat half crouched in the back of the white sports car, aware of perfume, heady and expensive, and aware of Carla's silver-gilt blonde head. They never touched, not once on the whole drive home. They had no need. With every word and gesture, Carla more than made it clear that theirs was a special intimacy which no one else could share.

The only surprise came when they got back to Milk River and walked into the hall. Someone— Adeline, Lindsey supposed: Adeline's touch was certainly there in the covered plate of sandwiches and thermos flask of coffee on the table beside the dying fire—had left all the lights switched on, and as Wolfe took the silver fox fur coat that Carla slipped off, Lindsey saw her clearly for the first time.

Had she never noticed or had she always previously seen her in poor light?—but as the overhead light poured down on her, Lindsey suddenly realised that Carla was much older than she had thought.

Wolfe was thirty-eight or nine—had he ever told her?—and she herself would soon be having another birthday that would put her on the downward line to thirty, but with the overhead shadows and the face somehow detached from its careful make-up, Carla, Lindsey saw, must be edging forty. Blonde hair and a petite, slim figure were deceptive, except in a hard light in the early hours of the morning.

'Do you want a nightcap?' Wolfe went across to the decanter beside the sandwiches on the table.

'No, I don't think so.' Carla yawned behind scarlet fingernails. 'I think maybe I'd just like to sit and talk a bit—have some intelligent conversation on which to go to bed. It's been a clod-hopping evening to say the least!' She smiled and curled herself up in a corner of the couch.

Everything she did was graceful, Lindsey acknowledged grudgingly. In spite of her scathing reference to Jan's party, Carla was as cool and unruffled as if the evening was still ahead of them and not come to an end.

A thought formed in Lindsey's mind. If Carla and Wolfe did marry, how would Carla take to motherhood? First the loss of that slender, supple figure, then the demands of a tiny baby and, after that, a toddler with small sticky hands clutching at her clothes and hair. All experiences that Lindsey longed to have, along with the love and laughter of a family of her own, but Carla looked too elegant, too self-absorbed, for the joys and sacrifices of raising children to have any great appeal. But then, Lindsey realised with a sickening jolt, with Milk River sold, there would be no need for Carla to make any sacrifice. She could have a childless marriage; she could have what she and Wolfe already had—a relationship with no official ties on either side. There was no need to provide an heir for an inheritance that belonged to someone else.

'Lindsey?' Wolfe was holding the decanter in her direction.

'No,' she said. 'No, thank you. I think I'll go straight to bed.'

The whole atmosphere cried out that she wasn't wanted, but Carla was still a guest and she forced a smile. 'Have you got everything you need?' she asked.

Carla paused before she answered, looking round with an expression of lazy contentment on her small, slightly triangular-shaped face. Was it her imagination or did the green eyes, colour heightened by the vivid emerald of her dress, rest fractionally on Wolfe before she finally replied?

'Oh, yes,' she answered in a throaty drawl. 'I think I've got everything I need!'

Of course she had! She had Wolfe and, for the crook of a little finger, she could have Milk River. What more was there to want? The sudden constriction in Lindsey's throat made it difficult to say good night.

'Good night, Lindsey.' Wolfe's voice stopped her halfway up the stairs.

She turned. A lock of hair had fallen like a comma across his forehead. He looked young and searching. He looked tender.

Her heart began to pump. This time, it was

her deliberately controlled voice that sounded icy.

'Good night!' She turned again and ran on up the stairs.

CHAPTER NINE

How did you sleep when all the time you were listening for the footsteps of the man you loved to pass your door on the way to his own room and never heard them no matter how hard you strained your ears?

Lindsey turned against the pillows and shut her eyes, desperate to blot out a picture of Wolfe with Carla in his arms either in the hall below or, worse still, in the big old-fashioned bed in the specially opened-up bedroom over the front porch and forced herself to think of nothing—certainly not her own future, which was such a meaningless blank.

One day soon, she supposed, if Milk River was going to be sold, she would have to make the effort and find another job and another place to live—but not yet. The humiliating truth was that, in spite of her earlier intentions, she couldn't leave. Not while Wolfe was there. Now that she had acknowledged she was in love with him, even seeing him with Carla was better than not seeing him at all.

She sat up suddenly, staring into the night, her heart thumping as if it had missed a beat. Someone had called her name—but that was ridiculous. Adeline was asleep, and had been for hours—and Wolfe was still with Carla. Exactly where they were, she refused to think.

It was hot, and she pounded at the pillow to make a cool place for her throbbing head. As she did so, she caught sight of her little bedside clock. The luminous hands said four-thirty, and yet she was quite sure it had been a little before four when she had last looked a few seconds earlier.

Oh, well—she lay back on her pillows with a thump—she must have been mistaken, that was all.

When she finally awoke, tired and gritty-eyed after a too short night in which dreams she could not pinpoint had constantly brought her to the edge of wakefulness before letting her slip back into another spell of heavy, unrefreshing sleep, the hands on the little clock stood at nine-thirty.

She didn't hurry—who would be about after such a late night?—and when she finally got downstairs, Adeline was backing through the swing door into the hall with a full tray set for breakfast.

'Here, let me help.' Lindsey caught hold of the door.

'Thanks.' Adeline edged her way past.

'Is the tray for Mr. Manston?'

'No!' Adeline was short. Breakfast was meant for the proper time; not halfway through the morning. 'The new boss has been up for quite a while. This is for Miss Morris.'

She stumped off up the stairs with a straight back and walked around the landing to Carla's room. From the way she knocked, Carla would be lucky not to get orange juice and waffles dumped in her lap. The thought brought the first smile of the day and, hard on its heels, came another one. If Carla was still in bed, Wolfe must be alone and she could have her breakfast with him. It was bittersweet, but

Lindsey was almost happy when she pushed open the kitchen door.

The room was empty. One place at the long table was still set, but the other had already been cleared away. Breakfast lost its charm and Lindsey was at the coffee pot, pouring herself a lukewarm cup, when Adeline banged back into the room.

'Where's Mr. Manston?' Lindsey carefully made the question casual.

'He's in the office.' Adeline started to work off her grievance about Carla's breakfast tray on the dishes in the sink. 'You're to go through when you're ready—but what about your breakfast, then?' she demanded as Lindsey left.

Lindsey could hear her grumbling on about 'waste of good food' and 'sleeping in with breakfast left to all hours' until the swing door shut behind her and she started to walk across the hall. At least Adeline was an ally against Carla—but then Adeline was reluctant to accept anyone who had had the misfortune not to be born and bred in Milk River. Anyone except Wolfe, that was.

It wasn't until she got to the door of the farm office that Lindsey stopped. What was she doing? Hurrying to see a man who had spent the night with another woman after making it perfectly clear exactly what his opinion was of you! Lindsey squirmed as she smoothed the tightly fitting waist of the blue cord dress she had put on in place of her usual working clothes.

What an awful thing love was! It robbed you of all pride and made you do things you never normally would. Crazy things like putting on a dress that made the pale blonde of your hair stand out in

sharp relief and tying your hair back with a matching bow, not tightly as usual, but softly so that it
framed your face. And once the hair was done,
taking blush and shadow and highlighting your eyes
so that they looked more midnight blue and smoky
without a trace of the redness left by a disturbed
night.

Even though you knew you could never compete
in looks with someone as classically beautiful as
Carla Morris, you did it just the same, and then you
threw pride to the winds and hurried so that you
could have just a little time alone with the man you
loved—even though you knew he was in love with
someone else and that your own love was mixed
with hate for what he planned to do.

It was hopeless, heartbreaking—and yet, for just
an instant when she opened the office door, it was
suddenly all worthwhile.

Wolfe had not heard her. He was sitting at the
desk, half turned in the swivel chair, with the
straight lines of his face and shoulders flowing on
into the leanness of his body. He was reading and
his head was bent; light coming through the window touched his hair and turned it to a thick, rich
ebony. He was absolutely still and so familiar—so
much the man she loved—that Lindsey's heart
caught in her throat.

She moved, and above a pale cream sweater and
tightly fitting pants, the head went back and turned
in her direction. 'How long have you been standing
there?' The light that had made his hair seem solid
now put what could have been a gleam of approbation in his eyes.

'Not long.' Nerves made her blunt and awkward.

'Adeline said you wanted to see me.'

'That's right.' The flicker in his eyes went out and his voice was as offhand as hers. 'I won't keep you if you're going out,' he glanced at the dark blue dress, 'but I wanted to discuss these.' He looked down at the papers he had been studying and Lindsey realised they were blueprints. 'I had the surveyor who came here draw them up, and it seems there's quite a lot of work to be done if the house is going to go on standing for another eighty years. Here, sit down.'

He reached over and pulled her desk chair up beside his own, forcing her to sit so close that she could smell the aftershave, see the fine grain of the skin and feel the warm touch of his breath against her cheek as he talked of pulling down and shoring up and returning the old house to the condition in which it had been when it was built. This time, however, there was to be a difference. Once rebuilt, Milk River was going to have Wolfe's stamp on it.

He might be going to sell, but there was always going to be a tangible reminder in the bricks and stones that another Wolfe Manston had once been at Milk River. That was his sense of continuity. That was to be his link with the first Wolfe.

'What do you think?'

How could he? How could he build and rebuild, just to sell and make a better price?

'I'm sorry.' He was talking to her. His face inches from her own, set and hard and steady. She might just as well try and change the course of the actual river that gave the ranch its name as try and change his mind or try and change her own reaction as she looked at him. 'I'm sorry,' she stuttered out again, 'I wasn't listening.'

His nostrils pinched above the straight line of his mouth. 'That much is obvious! What were you doing?' he asked with a bitter smile. 'Thinking about Foster? Wondering where he is?'

'Of course not!' She coloured furiously.

His eyes ranged over her. 'I wish I could believe it,' he said drily. 'Unfortunately, that's a little hard after last night.'

'I hardly knew that he was going to get drunk and pass out!' she protested.

'No,' he agreed, but the respite was minimal. 'What you did, however, know was that I would have preferred you to come with us.'

'And I preferred to go with a partner of my own choosing!'

'Yes,' he agreed, 'you did.' Then, totally unexpectedly, 'When is this going to stop, Lindsey?'

'I shall go on seeing Derek for as long as I like!' She confronted him with brilliant purple eyes. 'I only work for you, remember, you don't quite run my life!'

'I'm not talking about Foster, damn you!' On the desk his fingers clenched. 'I'm talking about us!'

'Us?' She couldn't believe her ears.

'Yes, us!' he repeated. 'We're Manstons, Lindsey, we've got a link, a bond, and yet ever since I arrived, you've fought me as if I'm not so much a stranger but an enemy!'

'When you're neither, I suppose!' He had brought her suddenly close to tears. The wild misunderstanding; the crazy fleeting thought that he had been talking about something other than the bloodline that they shared. 'What more do you want?' she demanded raggedly. 'You've got the ranch, the house, and I accept it. It should be yours—that's how things were laid down, and whatever you want to do with it, I know I can't change that. So what more do you want?' She was now more in control. 'That I should fall into your arms?'

'As a start, that might not be a bad idea.' He leaned back in his chair, openly taunting as his eyes went over her.

'And be told—what was it?' At that moment, she hated him for what he was doing to her. 'That I have the reflexes of a normal adult woman?' And every one of those reflexes was reaching out to him, remembering how it felt to be held against him and have his mouth come down on hers.

'Okay, Lindsey, let's stop playing games!' Control kept him leaning back and not shaking her by the shoulders. 'Let's behave like an adult man and a mature woman. Sit down!' he stopped her as she moved. 'For once you're going to stay and listen to what I have to say. I'm sorry about that incident—Okay, laugh if you like!' He couldn't know the effort behind that short, incredulous laugh. 'It wasn't what I meant to happen. It wasn't how I wanted things to be. God knows, to start with I didn't even want this place! I was happy as I was—no ties, no claims on my freedom, and then suddenly I'm told I've inherited not just a working ranch but people dependent on me for their livelihood. People like the Pinders and the Heshkas,' he sketched a gesture with his hands, 'and you! Do you realise that, when I came here, I didn't even realise you existed? Lindsey Kinsale was a boy; nothing else ever crossed my mind until you came through that door and—'

He had looked past her at the door. He had looked, but he did not look back. Drawn by his sudden stillness, Lindsey turned and saw Carla standing there.

'My dear, what passion!' Four words in a beguiling voice broke the moment into a thousand pieces. 'Good morning—once again!' Four more words told Lindsey everything.

Wolfe was behind her and Carla was in front. And Carla was beautiful. Suede trouser suit, blonde hair and brilliant emerald eyes; eyes that must have been vulnerable with sleep earlier that morning when Wolfe had forced himself to observe the proprieties and go back to his room. Lindsey had no need to see Wolfe's face: she knew.

'I'm not interrupting, am I?' Carla walked into the room; absorbing Lindsey but looking straight at Wolfe.

'No, of course not.' For the first time ever, Lindsey saw him at a loss.

'I'm going anyway.' Her words crossed his. 'I've got—' She stood up awkwardly. Wolfe had only momentarily been taken unawares. The control was back; the power as he also got slowly to his feet. 'I've got someone I have to see.'

'Lindsey!' His voice was warning as she went out, but she chose not to hear.

She was going over to the old Kersey place to get Annabel. Derek would be back by now. She would reclaim Annabel and leave. There was nothing she could do to save Milk River. How many weeks ago was it that John had told her that? Weeks in which she had stayed, pretending it was only for the contract which Wolfe had had drawn up, binding her to stay on as manager at the ranch.

Well, let Wolfe whistle for his contract; let him go to court for his ranch manager. She was leaving—leaving now! Or in just as long as it took to get Annabel and then get back and get her things. She would go to John and Jan, maybe, and Fire Bird— she remembered the chestnut mare in the barn outside—Fire Bird could stay until she had found a home and a new life.

Wolfe was hardly likely to take out any sort of retaliation on a horse and Fire Bird was not going to interfere with Carla's plans.

'You're not going to go out in this, are you?' Adeline was frankly disbelieving.

'Why not?' Lindsey zipped on her boots and took her sheepskin from the peg on the kitchen door.

'Because it's blowing a blizzard, that's why not! The weather advisories are out on the radio,' elbow-deep in flour for a new batch of bread, Adeline leaned on the dough on the kitchen table. 'Haven't you looked out of the window in the last hour?'

She had not looked out of the window or at anything except Wolfe since she had got up that morning. Wolfe and then Carla—and nothing, absolutely nothing, was going to stop her getting to the old Kersey place for Annabel and then getting right away: certainly not the stinging crystal ice that snow became as it blew into her face and hit the warmth of her unprotected head.

She turned up the collar of her sheepskin coat

and leaned into the arctic wind. She had a two-mile walk. The ground was flat, or almost, except where it went through clumps of bush, and going as the crow flew was by far shorter than following the road.

She was so cold when she finally reached the old farmhouse that her fingers in her sheepskin mittens hurt and it was agony to fumble with the latch as she tried to open the door. Her legs, in the skirt of the foolish dress rather than the protection of the pants she always wore when she went out in winter time, had lost all feeling soon after she had started out. The skirt of her sheepskin coat was long and had a good wrap, but the wind sliced up underneath.

Her legs had certainly been numb and feeling as if they belonged to someone else when she had stumbled through the final drift at the edge of the last patch of scrub and seen nothing where the farmhouse should have been.

For a moment, she had been convinced that somewhere in the swirl of blinding white behind her, she had taken a wrong turning, but then a particularly vicious gust of wind had blown the snow aside and she had just been able to make out the shape of the farmhouse a little off to the right.

Her half-sob of relief had made her realise just how frightened she had been. She had lived on the prairies for almost twenty years, but people who had lived there for the whole of much longer lives had been known to get utterly lost and die of exposure out here in wintertime. Only men like Jake, prairie born and bred and with a little something more that gave them the survival instincts of a deer or moose, could be called relatively safe.

But the sense of transient panic had stayed with
her as she had battled her way over the last hundred
yards and made her way more or less by instinct to
the farmhouse door. It was not until the latch finally
gave way under her scrabbling fingers and the door
blew open and dragged her inside that she became
less frightened than surprised. She was looking not
just at an empty kitchen, she was looking at an
empty house.

She had not been surprised that Derek had not
heard her—the wind would have whipped all sound
away as she wrestled with the door—but she was
surprised that he wasn't back.

She glanced at her watch. It was well past noon—
it had taken her more than an hour to make the
two-mile walk—and surely Derek should be back
by now. He would not have wanted to stay in
Saskatoon with John and Jan, any more than John
and Jan would want to keep him after the embar-
rassment of the previous night, and Annabel
should have been able to get through easily enough
on the highway.

The wind kept the main roads clear and scoured
and the snow settled in the ditches either side, not
on the black top. Derek should have been well
home by now, and the signs were that he had been.

The farmhouse had just two rooms downstairs;
the kitchen and the one Derek used as a bedroom.
Lindsay could see it through the open door. Draw-
ers had been pulled out and emptied and the closet
door was hanging off one hinge as if someone had
opened it in a hurry. There were other signs, too,
that someone—Derek—had been there and
packed and left. Clean patches on dusty surfaces

where small items had been removed. The typewriter she had loaned him was still there, though,
on the corner table—and there was a network
of still damp footprints going backwards and
forwards to the door.

Lindsey pulled on her mittens and turned the
collar of her coat up round her ears and made a
cautious circuit of the outside of the farmhouse.
Derek had obviously not just packed and left, he
had left in Annabel.

There was no sign of the little black car, and its
disappearance upset her to the point of futile tears.
Its loss hurt far more than Derek's abrupt departure, which left her surprisingly untouched. At one
time, she would have been desolate; now she no
longer cared. In fact, it was even a relief. It once
more seemed extraordinary that she could ever
have mistaken the superficial attraction he had
inspired for love.

She knew what love was now, though. An intensity of feeling that drowned out all other emotions; all, that was, except the fierce stab of
jealousy when you saw the man you loved
touching, looking, smiling at someone else.

She found a half-frozen tissue in her pocket and
blew her nose. She wouldn't think about Wolfe; she
wouldn't! What she would concentrate on instead
was getting back to Milk River, and this time there
would be no striking out across country, she would
go down the two grid roads, first south and then
west. It might be longer, but it was much safer than
risking getting lost in snow and scrub.

She was halfway along the first road from the
farmhouse when a vehicle appeared ahead, cut off

at fender height by the blowing snow. Her first thought was that it might be Annabel, but it was much too big. But then neither, she realised with a quick rush of relief, was it the big old Buick that had almost had her off the road when she had driven over the day before.

The day before! Was it really less than twenty-four hours since she had come across to ask Derek to Jan's party?

When she finally recognised the four-wheel-drive truck belonging to the ranch, it was almost alongside, inching its way through the snow with windshield wipers working furiously. Through the cleared glass triangle she could see Wolfe's face.

'Get in!' He leaned across and held the passenger door open against the wind. Lindsey hesitated; almost backed away. 'Get in!' he repeated.

She climbed reluctantly up into the warm cab, flinching with a sudden physical awareness as he once more leaned across and shut the door and his arm brushed up against her. She settled back into the corner of the seat, leaving a good two clear feet of space between them.

'Where the hell do you think you've been?' If she had ever thought she had seen him angry, she had been wrong.

His anger now was so complete and intense that it filled the confined space of the cab. The contrast of his fingers on the wheel, sensitive to every rut and stone as he turned the bulky vehicle on the narrow road, only heightened it.

'I asked you where you'd been!' Heading towards home, he put the question. His voice was quieter now but no less threatening.

Lindsey drew back even further in her corner. 'I don't have to account to you for what I do!' she said defensively.

'You do when—' The profile beside her tightened, leaving only a pulse spot beating at the corner of his mouth. 'You do when my housekeeper tells me that you rushed out of my house into the middle of a blinding snowstorm two hours ago and that no one's seen you since! And you most certainly do when I have Jake out combing the bush for you while I've been driving round the roads! Now,' a face incapable of laughter or tenderness was turned to her, 'for the last time of asking, where have you been?'

'I went to get Annabel.' Lindsey struggled to keep some defiance in her voice.

'To get your car, or because you couldn't keep away from that charlatan lover of yours?' Wolfe mocked her openly. 'Why didn't you take this truck if you needed to see him as badly as all that?'

She forgot the small surge of pleasure, almost hope, that had swept through her when she heard that he had cared enough to send Jake out looking for her while he searched the roads himself. 'Because I don't want to take anything that belongs to you!' she snapped.

'So you won't take anything from me, eh?' She saw him smile. 'It's a pity your boy-friend doesn't share your code of ethics! Where is Foster, by the way, and where's your car?'

'I don't know.' Lindsey bent her head and looked fixedly at her lap. 'Derek's gone, and I think he's gone in Annabel.' It wasn't Derek, it was everything—Wolfe, Annabel, Carla, the general hopelessness of it all—that put the catch into her voice.

She felt Wolfe glance at her. 'He'll come back,' he said brutally. 'That sort always does! At least by leaving now, he's saved me the trouble of going after him for his rent!'

His rent! That would be all Wolfe thought about. 'If he does come back, he won't find me here!' She knew it was childish, blurting it out like that, but suddenly she just had to get away. Annabel or not, she just had to get away from a situation that was more and more becoming one of exquisite torture.

'Oh, really?' There seemed no more than casual interest in Wolfe's voice as they turned in underneath the cross-pole of the wooden gateway that marked the entrance to the ranch. 'And why won't Foster find you here?'

'Because I'm leaving. Now—today!'

There was no reply. Instead Wolfe picked up speed and flatness went past on either side of them. A minute or two later, she could see the house, but he drove around the back and pulled up in the yard. For once, no Jake came running out to meet him. They were alone in their small island in a world of white. Wolfe switched off the engine. There was silence.

'So you're leaving, are you?' He sat watching snow fall on the windshield.

'Yes.' She watched it, too. Flakes funnelling down and bursting on the glass.

'I thought we had a contract.' Of course he would remember.

'Yes.' The contract which blind infatuation had let her allow Derek to persuade her to sign in an effort to establish some sort of claim on the estate. Claims, wills, ownership; how irrelevant and remote it all seemed now, sitting beside the man she loved and watching the snow falling.

'And I thought it had another three months to run.'

It did. Another three months in which Wolfe could marry Carla, sell Milk River, do anything he liked except keep her there to watch while it all happened.

'Yes,' she said, 'but I don't think you can enforce it.'

'Really?' He turned at last, thick hair just brushing the white sheepskin of his collar and grey eyes glinting behind black spiky lashes.

He could do anything, and he confirmed it.

'I shall do anything and everything it takes to keep you here!'

'Because of the Manston name? Because you're afraid I'm going to make it a laughing stock by chasing after Derek?'

'Maybe.'

Let him whistle for his contract! Let him whistle for his ranch manager for the next three months! She had thought it when Carla had come in earlier and she had hurried out of the farm office, and she thought it now, but much less firmly and with much less certainty.

'And now—' he leaned across. Subject closed; discussion over. He leaned across and calmly opened the truck door. 'You'd better go inside.' Cold struck her both from the open door and from his voice. 'Jake's out there somewhere looking for you and I want to go and tell him that you're safe.

Just because you choose to behave with such unbe-
lievable stupidity there's no reason for a man to risk
his life!'

Lindsey got out. Behind her the door slammed
and the truck was put into four-wheel-drive. By the
time she got to the kitchen door, it was going up the
swale behind the slough, bucking and lurching on
the snow. Some instinct for extra punishment made
her watch it until it disappeared.

Toller was watching, too; she could see the dog's
black face in the gap between the sliding barn door
and the frame. Even Toller had sense. On this, the
coldest day so far of the winter, Toller was not
stupid enough to come out across the yard.

Lindsey had never felt more isolated and alone as
she turned her back on the rapidly disappearing
truck and walked the last few feet to the kitchen
door.

It opened as she got there.

'So Wolfe found you, then?' Two women faced
each other. One smiling, self-possessed, with
nothing but a false concern dancing in emerald
eyes. The other miserable and cold, belonging
there but, in that moment, the outsider.

'Come in—you must be frozen!'

'Thank you.' Lindsey said it automatically as
Carla held the door.

Carla closed it carefully. 'Not at all,' she said.

CHAPTER TEN

FOR the next few days, Carla was everywhere, and there was rumour in the air.

As news of her presence spread in the tight-knit community, so did the word that the first wedding since Lindsey's mother had got married almost thirty years before could soon be taking place in the big house at Milk River.

They were wrong about the location, but as for the fact—each time, Lindsey tensed and clenched her teeth—who knew what Wolfe and Carla planned to do? Except sell Milk River; she was still sure of that.

She despised herself for staying on, using Wolfe's threat as an excuse, but she could neither change her feelings nor tear herself away, not even with Carla in every room, talking to Wolfe in her throaty voice, filling ashtrays with a succession of barely smoked cigarettes and occasionally looking from Lindsey to Wolfe and back again with an expression of enigmatic amusement in her shrewd green eyes.

Even when she was absent, a sense of her was always there. A scarf, maybe, or a pair of gloves left forgotten on a couch or a chair to bring a sudden, heart-clenching pang of misery. There was no escaping Carla, but worse, far worse, than the sight of her or of the possessions she left scattered so carelessly about was the thought of her alone with Wolfe each night.

The snowstorm ended as abruptly as it had begun, followed by an unseasonably warm spell that caused the snow on the shingle roof to melt each day and leave icicles like stalactites hanging from the eaves.

'She's not a picky eater, I'll say that for her.' Even Adeline was beginning to accept Carla. Even Adeline and even Jake—but then, what else had Lindsey expected? Carla was Wolfe's choice and Wolfe was 'the new boss'.

Lindsey looked woodenly down at the breakfast tray Adeline had brought in and put on the kitchen table. She couldn't speak through the hard lump in her throat and, behind Adeline, outside the window, an icicle left by the overnight sub-zero temperature blurred and danced in a million rainbow colours.

Carla had only to eat her breakfast—the coffee, juice and waffles with bacon and maple syrup that Adeline took up to her room every morning—to have Adeline begin to see her in a totally different light.

Would she be so approving, Lindsey wondered, if she knew that the big bed in the front bedroom had held two people until shortly before she had gone up with her tray? A dark head and a blonde one side by side on the queen-size pillows. And what would Adeline's reaction be—and Jake's—if they knew the future of Milk River—the future of their home—was in the balance?

She flicked damp lashes. 'Where's Miss Morris now?'

'Out.' Adeline put dishes in the sink. 'Didn't you

hear the car leave about ten minutes ago? Mr
Wolfe's taking her to lunch in Saskatoon and
they're stopping off at the Jarulsowskis' first. I
thought you knew that?'

Lindsey had known about the lunch, but not the
Jarulsowskis'. Carla was getting bored—that much
was obvious—and today's lunch was in the nature
of a bribe to get her to stay a few more days. Wolfe
was unwilling for her to leave without him and yet
reluctant, for some reason, to say his last goodbyes himself.

The blood of the first Wolfe running through his
veins must be stronger than she thought.

But Carla must be kept amused, and that meant
meeting everyone and being given a guided tour of
the house itself from roof to cellar the day before.
The Jarulsowskis—good Ukrainian stock who
hardly spoke any English in spite of a lifetime spent
in Canada—were probably the last novelty Wolfe
had to offer. When Carla had met them—and
started the sound of wedding bells ringing in Hettie
Jarulsowski's head—she would have met all the
Milk River tenants; exhausted everything life in the
prairies had to offer. There would just be the lunch
in Saskatoon and then nothing between Carla and
all the pressure she could exert on Wolfe to speed
up their departure.

'As they're going to be out, I thought I might go
into town myself.' Adeline meant Milk River, not
the larger centre. 'Will you be able to manage okay
for lunch?'

'Sure, I'll have a peanut butter and banana sandwich.'

Peanut butter and banana; the cure for all that

ailed her in all the years since Adeline had first
started making her lunchtime snacks.

Adeline shot her a sideways glance. 'There's
bananas in the cold store in the cellar.'

'Yes, I know.' Lindsey got up. Any minute now,
Adeline would be telling her that it wouldn't be so
bad if Wolfe married Carla.

Lindsey went through the office. She heard the
truck. Adeline had gone and she was alone. She
started to open the pile of letters she had earlier
driven down to the mail box to collect. It was easier
to concentrate, somehow, knowing that the door
was not going to open and Wolfe or Carla come into
the room.

It must have been on the second ring that she
heard the bell. So few people used the front door of
the house that it took a second for it to register.
It must be a rep from one of the seed firms or
agricultural machinery manufacturers, Lindsey
supposed, or another one of Wolfe's assessors
or surveyors.

She opened the door, and the first thing she saw
was Annabel. Framed in between two broad pairs
of shoulders and parked in the drive next to another
car which she had never seen before, it was defi-
nitely Annabel.

For the first time in days, Lindsey felt absolutely
and completely happy. The little old car had taken
on an importance way out of proportion to its
value. It and Fire Bird were the two things she
owned by right. Left over from the days when it had
seemed as if life was going to go on unchanged for
ever: before Ben Manston's sudden death and before the ranch's change of ownership.

The Mounties had been guardedly optimistic when she had reported the car missing, but she had never really expected to see the familiar black shape again. She had been sure Derek would abandon her in some out of the way place and that when finally identified, Annabel would be no more than an ancient heap of rusting metal.

'Ma'am!' The chunkier of the two men on the porch nodded enquiringly. 'Police—from Saskatoon,' he identified himself and his plain clothes colleague. 'If you're Miss Lindsey Kinsale, might we have a word with you?'

'Yes, of course.' Lindsey backed and left a space. 'Come in.'

'We were called to a disturbance in a hotel in Saskatoon last night, ma'am.' Explanations started and Lindsey almost didn't want to hear. 'Bit of luck, really. We'd been after his lordship—Foster, that is—for months, but he'd completely disappeared, dropped totally out of sight, and we'd just about given him up for lost when the call came through. He was trying to pass dud cheques again and he got into a fight. We've got him where he belongs now in the lock-up, but we thought we might as well bring the car back and get you to make a statement before we lay more formal charges.'

The second policeman produced a small black notebook and a pencil and sat ready to take notes.

Lindsey looked at him. 'But I don't want to lay any charges.' With Annabel back, Derek was over. Finished. Done.

'Really, ma'am?' The first officer looked

surprised. 'Oh, well, there'll be enough without that, I daresay.'

Lindsey frowned. 'What's he done?' she demanded quickly. 'What do you mean—there'll be enough without that?'

The two men looked first at each other and then at her. This was not the first time their meaning had had to be explained.

'I think you'd better sit down, ma'am,' the first one said.

Lindsey sat, and at the end of twenty minutes' patient explanation, she knew more about Derek Foster than she had ever known before. She also knew that practically everything Derek had ever told her about himself had been untrue. Everything except his name, that was.

'For some strange reason, he always sticks to that,' the first Mountie told her. 'Sometimes he'll use a phony British accent and call himself Sir or Lord, but he never uses any other name. It's almost as if he wants to get caught!'

'And he does—get caught, I mean?'

'Generally, only this time, I guess, the other side caught up with him a bit before we did. He'd been betting quite a bit and running bets for some mob in Toronto before he took off out here. The mob's goon squad was after him, so by and large, he was quite relieved when we came along and offered to lock him up in a nice, safe cell!'

'So it was all lies!' Lindsey remembered the big black Buick and the driver who had almost had her off the road. She also remembered the bruise on Derek's cheek and his obvious fear. 'The private school education, the wealthy background, wanting to leave Toronto so that he could write a book?'

'Hah!' The policeman laughed. 'The book's a new one, but otherwise we've heard it all before. Foster's a con man, ma'am, into anything. Bad cheques, kiting—that's using stolen credit cards for what you can get on them. He was a bit out of his league running with the Toronto mob. His speciality is latching on to lonely women and taking them for all they've got. He seems to have slipped up here, though.' Lindsey, in grey slacks and a white angora top, was given an approving look. 'It's always been older women he's gone for up till now—but I can quite see why he broke his pattern and chose you! I should take it as a compliment, if I were you, ma'am, and now you've got your car back, no harm done.'

She could also understand why Derek had chosen her, Lindsey thought, closing the door after the two police officers, but it was hardly for the reason either of them supposed. She might be younger than his victims usually were, but when Derek had first set eyes on her that day in the local store, to an experienced confidence trickster like him she must have seemed tailor-made.

Naïve, cut off, absorbed solely in the ranch—even the thought that she had seen partly through him, at least to the point where she had been relieved, not sorry, when he had taken off, was little consolation. She had been like someone living in another world. Derek had seen her for exactly what she was and exercised his not inconsiderable charm to make use of her. But it wasn't just the rent-free farmhouse, the money she had 'loaned';

Derek had done more to her than that. Without the infatuation that had passed for love with Derek, she might never have been ready to discover what real love was, and now, her whole body clenched, she not only had to face the prospect of losing Wolfe, she had to tell him that his reading of Derek's character had been absolutely right.

'Did you have a good day?' But she couldn't do it now. Not with Carla looking like the cat who'd stolen the cream, back from lunch in Saskatoon to one of Adeline's omelettes and a romaine salad, sitting next to Wolfe at the dinner table.

'Yes, quite.' Carla raised her wine and glanced over it, incongruous in the kitchen setting in her red dress.

Everyone from her uncle to old Jake Heshka in the yard had had their doubts aroused by Derek's plausibility and charm, and she had stubbornly ignored them all. Lindsey's cheeks flushed redder than Carla's red silk dress when she remembered the consequences of one particular denial. Wolfe telling her that Derek was a charlatan and thief and then taking her angrily in his arms.

'Your car's in the yard, I see.' Wolfe spoke and she felt the touch of his lips on hers.

'Yes.' She moistened them with her tongue. What a fool she was! 'Derek,' she stumbled slightly on the name and on her strict limitation of the truth, 'Derek arranged for someone to bring it back.'

'I see!' A masklike face with grey eyes narrowing, hardened even more.

'A gentleman to the last!' Carla's comment was not well meant.

'If we have seen the last of him.' Wolfe willed her
to answer him, making a question from a statement
and ignoring Carla sitting watchfully by his side.

'Who cares if we've seen the last of him or not?'
There was an edge to Carla's voice. 'I never met the
man, but from all I've heard, he was a total idiot.
Even Lindsey must realise that!'

In one stroke, she had done two things—re-
claimed Wolfe's attention and reduced Lindsey to
the status of a dull-witted child.

'Yes, maybe she does.' There was a last holding
of the eyes, grey into purple, and then Lindsey
looked away. 'Incidentally, I'll want you here
tomorrow.'

Lindsey's heart thumped painfully. 'Really?
Why?' she asked her fork.

'Because I've got the builders coming in,' said
Wolfe. 'I want to get the place fixed up before—' he
stopped. 'Before Carla leaves. They can do the
inside work now and then come back and finish off
outside when the warmer weather comes.'

This time, in a conversation of double meanings,
Wolfe had done two things—told her that Carla
would be staying on for days, maybe even weeks,
and that when he sold Milk River, Carla's mark
along with his would be stamped on it.

'Warmer weather!' Carla shivered inside her
dress. 'Don't mention it! I thought I'd freeze to
death when I woke up this morning. That room of
mine is like a mausoleum and the bed an Ice Age
museum piece!'

In other words—Lindsey went on playing word
games—warm enough when Wolfe was in it with
her but cold when he left to go back to his own room

in the servants' quarters before Adeline was up and about to see him.

A misery that started, then went on for the next few days as the Milk River Lindsey had always known disappeared under an invasion of tarpaulins and builders' scaffolding and something the same but subtly different reappeared as each stage of the work was finished.

Paint that had been brown turned white and Wedgwood blue and yellow. A new furnace was installed as walls came down—'My God, I'd almost forgotten what it was like!' Carla announced the following morning. 'I had a shower this morning and the water didn't run cold once in the whole five minutes!'

Carla was also in shirt and jeans that day, but a silk shirt and designer-monogrammed jeans. Those were her working clothes. Wolfe had suggested Carla supervise—a distraction to keep her occupied, stop her being bored and anxious to leave. Painters and decorators worked with an eye to Carla, not to Lindsey, and Lindsey had admit, grudgingly, that Wolfe's confidence was justified.

The biggest change was when an unconsidered alcove off the hall was turned, seemingly overnight, into a dining room. That was where the Wedgwood blue came in, with white panels picked out on the walls. The Colonial pine table admired so much by the young appraiser Wolfe had sent to value the contents of the house was cleared of books and journals and moved in from the hall, together with a buffet and six period chairs which Carla had somehow spotted in various parts of the house.

But then why shouldn't Carla have an eye for

interior decoration? As a hobby, it suited her. Rich, with no apparent need to work, Carla was not tied down by a job that demanded her attention almost twenty-four hours a day. She did not have to go out to the Heshkas' or the Pinders' on demand, no matter what the weather, to deal with petty emergencies, nor did she have to live through the refined torture of seeing the man she loved look straight at another woman whenever he came into a room.

But Wolfe was looking straight at her one morning a week later. He had been out; cold clung to his hair and to his face and throat as he stripped off his sheepskin coat and threw it on the nearest chair with one dismissive sweep.

'I've been down for the mail.' All cold was comparative. His voice was colder than the coldest freezing point.

'I—' Lindsey cleared her throat, 'I was meaning to drive down later.' She spoke to the dull bronze sheen of skin in the open collar of his shirt. For once, she couldn't run. She was alone with him; something she had avoided being for days. When he had stayed indoors, she had found errands to take her out. When he was out, she had hidden herself away, now they were here, face to face or, more accurately, his face to the top of her bent head, and he was holding out a letter in front of her.

'This is for you.'

'Thank you.' She took the letter in the cheap blue envelope.

He had handed it to her reverse side up, and the first thing she saw was Derek's name. Derek's name with a return address written on the back.

'You don't seem surprised.' He was accusing, even threatening, as her head went back. A pulse beat in the angle of his jaw and his eyes were like cold steel.

'I didn't . . .'

'. . . think he'd come back?' Wolfe finished for her. 'I think I told you once.' He paused and studied her; not moving, breathing, but just holding her with the sheer force of his look. 'His sort always does. Open it, Lindsey. See what he says—but,' he turned abruptly and went towards the door, 'don't let him come near me!'

He went, and Lindsey stood there motionless. Her heart had to settle down and her pulse resume its normal rate before her fingers could function or her mind could think.

She turned the letter over in her hands, tempted not to open it. She had still not told Wolfe the full story about Derek, denying it to herself as much as Wolfe that she had been deceived and used in Derek's pursuit of money. But now Derek had come back into her life and not opening the letter would make no difference. He was back, something to be faced, and she had better do it now.

She ripped the envelope open and a printed slip fell out and fluttered to the floor. She let it go. It was the letter that interested her. It was written on cheap, lined paper with the full address of the Regional Correctional Centre and Derek's name and a prison number in the top right-hand corner.

He was sorry, Derek said. He was sorry for what he'd done and he'd like to see her and explain. That was why he had enclosed a visiting order. He hoped she would drive down and see him. He had no one else to ask and he would be waiting for her every day at visiting time.

Lindsey picked up the printed slip and looked at it, almost ready to crumple it up and throw it away. Prisoner 8270 Foster D. had permission for one visitor—Miss L. Kinsale—to make one thirty-minute visit between the hours of two and four any weekday afternoon within the next fourteen days, after which the order would expire.

Much though she wanted to ignore it, the thought of Derek waiting—expecting her every afternoon—began to play on Lindsey's mind. In spite of everything, it was pathetic to think of him sitting behind bars, waiting and waiting, all his pretensions stripped away and face to face with the real truth about himself at last. Lindsey kept finding herself re-reading the letter. There was no hint of his old confident manner or of his grandiose dreams of life as a famous writer. The letter itself was painful, with simple words misspelled and badly formed as if the writer was unaccustomed to even holding a pen. For all his talk about being a best-selling novelist, Lindsey realised, in real life, Derek was barely literate.

The inevitability that she would make the visit grew as February came to an end. The spell of unseasonably warm weather had been followed by a biting snap of cold. The sun shone in a clear blue sky, but with so little warmth that the ice coating every exposed surface was never touched but stayed as rigid and unyielding as Wolfe had become ever since the arrival of Derek's letter. If once she had thought him distant and absorbed, for all the notice he now took of her, she might not have been there at all.

It was different with Carla, though, Lindsey thought early one morning when, muffled to the ears, she was standing in the yard, wrestling with the plugs in Annabel's engine which, like everything else around, seemed to have turned into blocks of solid ice. Wolfe might ignore her, but for Carla there was always time. Probably because Carla was becoming increasingly irritable and bored now that the work in the house was almost done, and even Wolfe was finding it hard to keep her there.

'Darling, I know I'm only a sleeping partner, but I do have work to do—and besides, if I don't get back east to civilisation soon, I think I'll go quite mad!' The comment, half unintelligible and half quite clear, was made early one evening when Carla was sitting beside the blazing fire.

'Just a few more days, love, and then I'll be able to come with you,' Wolfe had coaxed her. 'Tell yourself the break is good for you.'

'Like hell it is!' But Carla had raised her dry Martini glass and toasted him.

Wolfe had gone then and a silence settled, broken only by the hiss of air escaping from the logs. Lindsey went to put her own glass on the small side table, and Carla jumped.

'Goodness,' she exclaimed, 'you startled me! I'd forgotten you were here!'

'I'm sorry.' Pressing on to her own self-destruction, Lindsey went rashly on. 'Perhaps you would prefer it if I left completely so that you and Wolfe,' she stumbled slightly, 'can have the whole place to yourselves?'

'Don't be ridiculous!' Carla studied her impatiently. 'Whether you leave or not is of absolutely no consequence. Wolfe and I have known each other far too long and far too well for anyone to come between us now.'

She opened her flat gold case and took out a cigarette. There was silence as she lit it and sat gazing through the smoke.

Left standing there, Lindsey wondered why she was so upset. Carla had told her no more than she already knew—had known—ever since that night on the telephone, before Carla had even set foot in Milk River. And since then, every minute of every day had only served to emphasise the closeness she had with Wolfe. Why then, if she had always known it, did it have to hurt so much to hear the truth put into words?

Carla leaned towards the ashtray on the sofa table. She stubbed out her cigarette and her eyes swept across Lindsey's face. 'Oh, no,' she repeated quietly, 'it's not you that bothers me. It's this place.'

'Milk River?'

'Yes, Milk River,' Carla mimicked. 'This stretch of nowhere buried in the back of beyond! It's bad enough in itself, but now Wolfe's got to go and get this crazy idea that he belongs here!'

'It happens to be his home.' For as long as Wolfe chose to keep it, Lindsey added silently.

'If you subscribe to the principle of ancestor worship which, quite frankly, I don't, I suppose you could say it was his home!' Carla retorted. 'But what about his work? What about the Marc LeBret side of his life? For as long as I've known him—and that's about ten years now—Wolfe Manston's never been interested in settling in one place. He's always been just going somewhere or just coming back. The world's his home. He's a travel writer and a damned good one at that, and now he's throwing it away for the sake of some misguided sentiment! But still,' her taut face relaxed and she reached for another cigarette, 'I guess I can afford to wait for the novelty to wear off. I know Wolfe, I know him very well.' Carla's confident smile and the click of her lighter plucked at Lindsey's nerves. 'It won't be long before he can't get away fast enough!'

A last hope that she had been wrong, that Wolfe was not planning to sell the ranch, flickered and died. Carla had aroused it with her talk of Wolfe thinking of Milk River as his home and Carla had squashed it just as quickly as it had arisen. Carla was against it and—looking at Carla now as she sat there, smoking, and gazing dispassionately around the newly decorated hall in which she had had such a hand—Lindsey knew that Carla would always win.

'Here, let me do that!'

Two mornings later, in the yard, Wolfe's totally unexpected voice sent the wrench spinning and clattering from her mittened hands while the plugs in Annabel's engine stayed firmly put.

He had come up close behind her without a sound—or else she had been so immersed in her thoughts that she had not heart him—and he was standing, legs slightly apart, hands thrust into his pants pockets and head a little on one side above the bulk of a thick wool sweater. He was even smiling—at least, there was a lightness in his eyes, and the finely shaped mouth held the suspicion of a quirk, but when Lindsey straightened from picking up the wrench, she was armoured against his smile, his look, his charm.

'It's okay, I can manage, thank you.' Her breath touched him in a frozen plume and underneath the bare, dark head, the eyes began to narrow.

'What are you doing?' His voice, once warm, was neutral.

'Putting a new set of plugs in Annabel.'

'I didn't know you had so many hidden talents!' He was inviting her to respond; inviting her, as he had once put it, to stop fighting him. Lindsey just stood there. 'Anyway,' she had lost her chance; his tone was frigid and off hand and his face held only cursory interest, 'where are you going? At least, I assume you're going somewhere as you're not in your working clothes.'

He glanced down at pale blue trouser legs; she had her light blue pants suit on under her sheepskin coat. And, irony of ironies, she suddenly realised, Derek had been with her when she had gone shopping and *he* had made her buy that suit.

'Yes, I'm going to Regina. I have to see—' she began belligerently but her courage petered out when it came to Derek's name, '—a friend.'

'I see.' Wolfe began to turn dismissively away. 'In that case, take the truck or your uncle's car. They're both more reliable than this.' Annabel was equally dismissed. 'I shan't be needing them. I'm driving Carla back to Saskatoon.'

He said it with the back of his head towards her,

already walking away. Ten strides later and he was at the kitchen door. It opened and closed behind him and he was gone.

For good, she wondered, or just for the day? Was he only driving Carla to Saskatoon or was he flying on with her? Had Milk River begun to bore him even more quickly than Carla had predicted and allowed her to persuade him to leave?

Questions, questions, questions but no answers, either in her head or in the empty, frozen yard. Only Wolfe knew the answers to those questions and there was no way she could now run after him and ask. Her only option was to go and visit Derek and then wait and see when she got back.

CHAPTER ELEVEN

WHEN she did get back, it was almost midnight and the house was in total darkness. A perversity she had recognised as stupid had spurred her on to change the faulty plugs and set off in Annabel rather than in either one of the ranch's more reliable vehicles and her perversity had cost her hours. Annabel had repaid her by behaving like a temperamental prima donna all the way.

The city of Regina was to the south, much farther south, heading towards the province of Alberta and the border with the United States, and the return journey had taken her well over twelve hours just for a thirty-minute visit with Derek.

And it had been an agonising thirty minutes. The Correctional Centre was depressing, and Derek was more depressing still. In spite of the prison clothes, in spite of the prison walls, he still clung to a pose of injured innocence and to the story that he was one day going to write a book.

The letter had been honest—well, as honest as he could get—but face to face, it seemed impossible for Derek not to put on an act. And what was so depressing was that she had once been so naïve that she had believed the talk and the phoney charm and glamour.

Derek would never change, she thought on the long drive back, because he was unwilling to face up to reality, but reality was the only thing she had left to face if she was not, like Derek, to waste her life.

It was true she loved Wolfe—perhaps she always would—but Wolfe had Carla and another life, another life under another name, which included neither her nor Milk River. Whatever his plans were for the ranch, it could never be her home again. It was Wolfe's to dispose of as he wished. It belonged to him and, through him, it belonged to Carla.

The smoke was there from Carla's cigarettes; faint but there in every room and overlaid with a slight hint of the perfume she always wore.

It was the first thing Lindsey noticed when she got back. She could change the darkness by switching on every light, but she could not dispel the sense of Carla's presence.

The house was empty, and its very emptiness showed how unimportant she was to Wolfe. He had left without a word. He had gone to Saskatoon with Carla and then they had both flown on.

Adeline was also out. A note stuck to the fridge with a small magnetic holder announced that she had gone into town to spend the night with her sister, but there was nothing from Wolfe. Lindsey looked first in the kitchen and then in the farm office, but there was nothing. No note, no message written in his boldly slanting script, to confirm her intuition that Carla had been right. Milk River and its novelty had begun to pall and Wolfe had flown back with Carla to Toronto and the life they shared.

Lindsey closed the door on the farm office, walked back through the hall and the silent kitchen and went up the back stairs to her room. What more did she need to tell her that to stay on at Milk River would compound her misery? She had to leave and she had to do it now, before Adeline came back in the morning and demanded explanations.

Apart from Annabel, Fire Bird was the only thing she had left from her old life, and she could make arrangements for Fire Bird later on. For now, she just had to get away, throw a few things into a bag and drive on to Saskatoon and a motel. She walked along the passage to her room and switched on the light.

The footsteps terrified her. She was packing when she heard them; slow and measured, making an almost supernaturally loud noise in the otherwise empty house. She froze above her half-packed bag as if by very will she could force them to go away.

'What do you think you're doing?' It couldn't be, but the harshness in Wolfe's voice behind her was real enough. It couldn't be, because Wolfe was in Toronto—he wasn't here. He was back in his own environment with Carla and the life they shared, unless, of course—a sickening certainty made Lindsey cold—their plane had been delayed or cancelled and Carla was downstairs. Very, very slowly Lindsey turned in the direction of the voice.

'I asked you what you were doing?' He was wearing the same white sweater in which she had last seen him that morning, but all the shadows of the house were gathered in his eyes.

For a second, her whole being reached out to him. 'I'm leaving because I love you!' her heart pounded. 'I'm leaving,' was all she said in a hard, flat voice.

'I see.' He seemed barely interested as he walked into the room, even stopping to pick up a book that she had tossed on to the bed in her hurry to be away. It was one of his, one of a set she had had sent in, all of them published by the prestigious Toronto publishing house of Carl Feinster. He glanced at the title and put it back.

'Jake and Adeline should be able to manage here for the next few weeks,' Lindsey hurried on to break the silence.

'The next few weeks?' His head snapped sharply back and he looked at her. 'What have the next few weeks got to do with it?'

She tried to look away but couldn't. 'Until you sell,' she said.

'Until I *what*?' She had never seen him taken totally by surprise. 'You're not saying you still believe that nonsense?'

She had, however, seen him angry and contemptuous.

'Why shouldn't I?' She picked up something— anything—and rammed it in her bag. 'You've never told me that I'm wrong!'

'Stop that!' His hand came out and gripped her wrist. 'I didn't think I had to tell you,' he said roughly. 'I thought you understood what I feel about this place. All right,' his fingers tightened as she turned her head away, 'don't listen, but for God's sake, Lindsey, listen to your senses and hear what they have to say! Don't they tell you anything, or are you so bound up in Foster that you're blind to everything unless it has to do with him?'

'Derek has nothing to do with this!' Lindsey pulled her wrist away. What need had she to listen to her senses? They were so acute that the mere touch of his fingers sent a mindless longing spinning through her brain.

'Doesn't he?' His words brought her back to earth, made the floor firm against her feet and filled the weightless void. 'In that case,' dark lips brushed breath across her cheek, 'why did you spend the whole day visiting him? Oh, don't look so surprised!' Dark lips snapped into a thin, straight line. 'I made it my business to find out about Foster weeks ago. Was he pleased to see you?' he demanded harshly. 'And what have you arranged?' He broke off to glance at the half-packed bag. 'That you should get an apartment near the prison and play the part of the devoted wife until he's released? Who knows?' No one had ever looked at her as Wolfe was looking at her now. 'If Foster can ever reconcile himself to the fact that you're not a rich heiress, you might even be able to persuade him to turn make believe into fact one day! I'm quite sure you've already shown him the pleasures he could expect!'

Lindsey's hand instinctively went back, then dropped. Wolfe was attacking her with words and she could use the same.

'How dare you?' she bit out. 'How dare you accuse me of having an affair with Derek, when all the time your mistress is downstairs!'

'My mistress?' Even with words, she couldn't beat him. He was smiling, actually smiling, as he answered her. 'If by mistress you mean Carla, then you're wrong. She's in Toronto . . .'

'Having decided that Milk River bores her?' Lindsey fought to extinguish the tiny flame of hope. 'In that case, I'm surprised that you came back!'

'Are you?' Wolfe was suddenly and surprisingly quite calm. 'Then let me tell you. I came because I thought there was a question to be asked and a decision made. I think, however, that the last few minutes have made them both unnecessary.'

He was at the door before she found the courage. 'Wolfe, I've got to know. Please tell me!' Her voice faltered. 'About Milk River . . . ?' It trailed away.

He stood for what seemed an hour, a rigid figure in the doorway filled with tension and total stillness.

'If I told you anything now,' he said scathingly, 'would you believe me?'

Lindsey was still there, still on the spot where Wolfe had left her, when the sound of the kitchen door opening and closing took her to her bedroom window. He was walking across the yard towards the rented car. So he was leaving—Lindsey felt sick and cold—but he opened not the driver's but the passenger door, and when he straightened up, he shut the door and turned back towards the house.

The last person she had seen was Jake, a tiny dot way off in the bush, setting trap lines maybe, or just going about his own personal business.

The only person she had spoken to that morning was Adeline, who had come back from spending the night with her sister when Lindsey was getting into Annabel.

'Where are you going?' Adeline was surprised.

'Into town.' It was accurate enough. Adeline

would assume she meant Milk River, and Adeline couldn't see the bag in Annabel's trunk that she had packed to go to Saskatoon.

'You're early.' Yes, she was. She had been determined to be up and off before Wolfe had even woken up, far less left his room. 'Nothing'll be open!' Adeline frowned and, for all her rationalisation, Lindsey felt terrible.

She should be making her goodbyes; telling Adeline she would not be coming back. Instead, she prevaricated by glancing at her watch. 'They will be by the time I get there.' And that was certainly true enough. All the stores in Saskatoon would be open and doing business by the time she had driven there. 'Take care!' Lindsey put the car in gear and drive away. Take care, Adeline, she said underneath her breath.

Adeline, the house, Fire Bird—there but invisible in her stall in the barn—grew smaller in the mirror. She would take the grid roads to Saskatoon; the unpaved side roads that were rarely used. She was sneaking away like a thief from her own home; the back roads were appropriate.

She passed the old Kersey farmhouse Derek had rented and, way off in the distance, the dot she recognised as Jake straightened and looked in her direction. He would be curious about a car on these roads in wintertime, but she was probably too far away for him to be certain it was Annabel, just as she would not have been certain it was Jake if it had not been for the brilliant red dot of the woolly toque he always wore.

Annabel's studded snow tyres bit into the two-inch covering of ice and snow on the narrow dirt and gravel roads, and, as if to make amends for her stop-and-start behaviour of the previous day, the little car was running like a dream. Lindsey drove along, half concentrating on her driving and half thinking.

Wolfe would probably be up now, wondering where she was. He would doubtless have things to do that would require the presence of his ranch manager, unless he was already on the telephone—her heart gave a painful thump—making arrangements to catch the next flight east. And even if he did come after her; even if he had been telling the truth about Carla and his feelings for his heritage, he would assume she had gone south to Derek and Regina and not west and a little north to Saskatoon.

But why think of Wolfe when she should be thinking of her own plans? Lindsey stepped on the gas and Annabel picked up speed. She would go to John first—maybe stay with him and Jan—and John could call Adeline and let her know that she was safe. The confidentiality that existed between a lawyer and his client should make it easy for John to refuse to give details of her whereabouts, and, in that breathing space, she would start thinking about the best way to re-start her life.

A life as far away from here as possible. One that—Annabel started to shimmy across the road. Lindsey turned the wheel, but it seemed to have no connection with the drive shaft and Annabel just went smoothly on, sideways towards the ditch. Ice and snow had built up in her tyres and she was skating.

There was a jolt, a lurch, and then the world stopped moving and tilted at a crazy angle. With a long sigh, Annabel stopped and settled hood down in the ditch.

Damn! Lindsey left the engine running and got out and walked around the car. There was a two or three-inch gap between the back wheels and the side of the road. Everyone with any sense carried a shovel in the trunk of their car in winter, but a shovel was no use now. To drive out, Lindsey saw, she would have to dig right down into the ditch until Annabel's point of balance shifted and her back wheels came down. Getting her out was a job for a tractor, not a shovel and—Lindsey looked around the flat, white emptiness—there was little chance of a tractor magically appearing here.

She had driven far enough to have left Milk River property, but there must be a farmhouse of some sort a few miles on. She went back, switched off the engine, pulled on woolly hat and gloves and hunched her shoulders and neck deeper into her sheepskin coat. She could walk. She could do it easily. She had to get away, and nothing was going to stop her now.

She had gone perhaps a hundred yards when she realised how cold she was. She was walking into the wind and her face was already so numb that frostbite was not a chance but a probability. She stopped. She was letting her need to get away override common sense. Her feet invisible in the snow blowing across the road at ankle height, she turned around and went back.

'Don't run the risk of dying from exposure. Stay in the car and wait for someone to come along.' She heard the warning almost every day on the radio, and it now applied to her. She forced herself to be rational. She had a blanket, candles, matches and some chocolate—all part of the winter survival kit that, along with rope and shovel, Jake automatically put into all the ranch vehicles every fall.

She would be warm; she would survive, and someone would come along.

She sat there, huddled in her blanket. She would keep the chocolate and the extra clothes in the bag in the trunk until later; she tried not to think how much later. She switched on the radio; she might as well have company until the car's battery gave out. Her breath froze and frosted up the windows and she sat in her white world and listened.

'This Week With Books.' The music stopped and a man's voice came through. 'The programme this week explores the relationship between the author and his publisher.' Lindsey tensed. She had often heard the programme, but this was too close to Wolfe. 'Often a turbulent relationship,' the interviewer was going on, 'but certainly not in the case of Canada's best-selling Marc LeBret and his publisher, Carla Morris, daughter of the late Carl Feinster and now head of the publishing house her father founded.'

'No, indeed!' Shock made Carla's distinctive voice seem distant. His publisher—Carla was Wolfe's publisher! The throaty voice got louder as the shock waves died away and Lindsey's ears began to work again.

'We've always had a good relationship with Wolfe since we published his first book ten years ago,' Carla was now saying, 'and we intend to keep it just that way for many years to come.'

'Wolfe?' The interviewer queried through

Lindsey's bitter little smile. The phrase 'a good relationship' could cover many things.

'Marc, then!' Carla sounded impatient. 'But at Feinster's we like to think of ourselves as one big family, and that means first names and not pen-names or pseudonyms.'

'A perfect introduction to the man behind the scenes,' the radio staff man slipped in smoothly. 'Wolfe Manston, known as Marc LeBret to millions of armchair travellers around the world, and now with a new book about Australia out on the shelves.'

'Out today, in fact.' Wolfe's voice filled the car, and Lindsey gripped the steering wheel until her knuckles whitened.

'This programme is being recorded in Marc LeBret's apartment in a luxury block right in the heart of downtown Toronto.' Lindsey once more tuned in to the interviewer's smooth voice. 'On the same floor, in fact, as the apartment belonging to his publisher.' Carla began to talk, but the man quickly overrode her, bringing Wolfe into the conversation. 'Quite a change from some of the more remote places you've been to for your work, no doubt?'

'Yes, but a contrast that won't be applying for too much longer.' Lindsey heard the words but not their meaning.

On the same floor as Carla's; an apartment on the same floor as Carla's. Not theirs but his— Wolfe's. And in apartment blocks—in luxury apartment blocks—there was often a private telephone exchange acting both as answering service and a buffer between the outside world and residents who, to afford the rents, were not only rich but often famous.

Lindsey's thoughts raced wildly on, connecting disconnected words and phrases. The whole premise on which she had based her false assumption had been wrong. Wolfe and Carla did not share a telephone—their calls were made through the same telephone exchange—and Wolfe and Carla did not share an apartment. If only she had asked when Wolfe had handed her that piece of paper with his telephone number on it and she had recognised it as the one Carla had also given her; if only she had not jumped to the conclusion that Carla was his mistress.

'It must have been a difficult decision.' But it was too late for 'if only's'; Lindsey barely heard the conversation continuing on the radio.

'No.' Wolfe's voice claimed her full attention. The whole atmosphere of the interview had changed, she realised; she could feel it, even through the air waves. Until then, it had been smooth and superficial, but now, with Wolfe talking, it was no longer superficial but serious, deadly serious, and Wolfe wasn't talking about any relationship with his publisher or even about his latest book, he was talking about Milk River. 'Sure it's a commitment, but it's not one it's hard to face. It's where my roots are and it's where I and my wife are going to live.'

'Your wife?' For a second, the interviewer faltered. This was a piece of information that had not been included in his pre-broadcast notes. 'But you'll still go on travelling for your work, of course?'

'Not as Marc LeBret.' Wolfe was adamant. 'If there's any more travelling to be done, it will be done by Wolfe Manston and his wife. I've spent my whole life going from one place to another, searching out new experiences, when what I was looking for was here in Canada all the time. I've found the home I never knew I had and the only woman with whom I could ever think of sharing.'

Lindsey's heart stopped. It literally and absolutely stopped.

'Actually,' the sound of his smile, the sudden picture of his face, made it beat again, 'I was a little premature in calling her my wife. It won't be until I get out West again that I can ask her to marry me!'

'Darling, you can't be serious!' Carla sounded stunned. It was good radio; no wonder the off-the-cuff remark had been left in. Surprises were being sprung in the course of an actual interview.

'Quite serious.' Wolfe spoke again. 'I had to wait until this book was finished, but I've known exactly what I wanted to do for the last few months. I can pinpoint the moment, if you like.' A voice just touched with French grew softer and slate grey eyes were luminous in a tender face. Lindsey could see it—feel it—even through the radio. 'It was when a stubborn, angry girl with hair the colour of winter wheat was riding hell for leather on a horse likely to throw her at any second and I realised that if it did—if anything happened to her—there would always be an emptiness in my life.'

She knew the moment. She had been galloping down the slough to the old Kersey place, desperate

to get Wolfe's first meeting with Derek over wi
but even more desperate to throw off the effect
the man galloping to overtake her.

Why had she denied it—why had she nev
guessed?

'And now, as it seems a day for confession
here's another one.' Wolfe had taken charge of tl
interview. 'This book about Australia is going to l
the last one Marc LeBret will ever write!'

'Wolfe . . . !' Carla was warning him, but Wol
was deaf.

'Until now, writing has always been the mo
important thing in my life,' he went firmly on. 'No
the most important thing will be my home an
marriage, and neither has any place for Ma
LeBret.'

'So Marc LeBret gives way to Wolfe Manst
and, hopefully, a new output of work!' The inte
viewer, with years of practice, filled the gap.

'Hopefully, indeed!' Carla took up the lead, b
Lindsey was no longer listening.

Millions might have heard him, but Wolfe ha
been talking just to her. He had been telling h
that he loved her and had done so almost since the
met. There had never been an affair with Carla-
her spirits soared—and even if there had, all tha
mattered now was that Wolfe loved her, loved he
loved *her*! Everything was going to stay the sam
There would be sons to carry on the tradition
Milk River, their sons, hers and Wolfe's; nothin
was going to change.

But—euphoria hit the shock of cold reality—sh
was sitting in a snowbound car miles from any
where, and she had left him. Wolfe would think sh

had gone to Derek—who would know *where* she had gone? She had left no clue, no trace, as to her destination.

By the time anyone came along this isolated road, it could well be too late. Too late for her to get home that night and too late—perhaps for ever—to convince Wolfe of her longing to be his wife.

She scraped her frozen breath from the windshield. The surrounding prairie was just as white and empty, but the sky seemed even lower and greyer than it had. There was music again on the radio, and she switched it off and tried the engine. If it started and she ran it sparingly, she could at least keep warm.

It was only when the shadow of a man fell across her window that she knew anyone had stopped. Forgetting about the engine, she scrabbled at the handle in the door with clumsy, half numb fingers, desperate to get it open and be taken back to Milk River.

The door gave, but not to her desperate fingers. It was wrenched open from outside and, for a second, Lindsey sat there, gazing up at Wolfe.

'Thank God I've found you! Thank God Jake was right!' Wolfe pulled her out into arms that felt as if they would never let her go and she was laughing, crying, still feeling the warm pressure of his lips against her face and throat when he finally released his hold and held her at arm's length.

'Are you okay?' His eyes, too, were brilliant; his mouth hard to control. She nodded; more tears came spilling over and she was pulled back against his chest. 'Come home, my love,' he whispered. 'Come home, my love, come home!'

CHAPTER TWELVE

'I WANT to hear you say you believe me.' A new Wolfe, younger, happier, more tender, raised his face from hers.

Flames leaped behind him, irregular as the beating of her heart. 'Of course I do!'

They were in the hall, together on the couch. Adeline had gone off to her sister's. Gone? Sent? Lindsey had no way of knowing. Both Adeline and Jake had been there when Wolfe had brought her back, overwhelming in their relief and with their questions, but when she had come downstairs, warm from a bath and dressed in her blue velour robe, Wolfe had been there alone to wrap her fingers around a steaming glass and make her drink its contents, and the house was empty except for the two of them.

'Then say it!' he commanded. 'No more nonsense about believing I'm going to sell Milk River! No more Foster!'

Above her, the jawline tightened and she raised her hand and touched it. 'And no more Carla!' she teased him softly.

'Lindsey . . . !' It came out fiercely.

'No, Wolfe, don't tell me. I don't want to know.' There *had* been something more with Carla. A long time ago, maybe, way back in the ten years Carla had mentioned on the radio, but there had been more than an author-publisher relationship.

'Darling . . . !' She arched her head back on her neck in invitation but Wolfe ignored it.

'No!' he said almost curtly. 'It's confession time and this time you're not going to stop me. I'm thirty-eight and I've never had a settled home or lived in one place for more than two years at a time. Women have always been something to meet—or not!—when I got off the plane and then say good-bye to when I got back. I'm thirty-eight, I've never had a permanent relationship and, as of now,' he gave a rueful smile and the new Wolfe—her Wolfe—briefly reappeared, 'I'm unemployed! I'm mad—that's what Carla would say—did say!—and I'm asking you to marry me. And you'll be mad as well if you agree!'

'I'm twenty-five. Not too old to have a child, but—' her heart clenched as she looked into his face, 'unless it's yours, there won't be any child. As for Carla—' She knew—oh, how she knew— exactly what Carla must be feeling. She had had her own experience of being on the outside looking in, and now Carla was in Toronto, in her apartment, on her own. 'And as for unemployment,' Lindsey changed what she had been going to say, 'you've a ranch to run and sons to raise, because,' she once more arched her neck and, this time, Wolfe did not ignore her invitation, 'when I've given you your sons, I'm going to be busy having daughters!'

She finished in a muffled whisper, her voice vibrating against his lips.

'Darling—take me to bed!' She had had no idea she could give or get such dizzying pleasure as his mouth moved down her throat towards her breasts.

'I plan to—soon!' He moved and suddenly her

head was against his shoulder and she was no longer looking at the crisp thick darkness of his hair but at a face filled with the tenderness of gentle laughter. 'First, however, I intend to have a contract.'

'For a ranch manager?'

'No.' He moved easily against her weight and she heard the crackle of the paper he took out of his pocket.

'What is it?' She stared blankly up at the sheet of print and then into his eyes.

They danced, grey lights moving behind her own reflection. 'A special marriage licence!'

Lindsey drowned in those grey lights as his mouth came down to claim her.

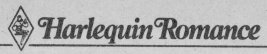
❧ Harlequin Romance

Coming Next Month

2755 CINDERELLA WIFE Katherine Arthur
The idea of pretending to be the adoring wife of a powerful
fashion mogul is bizarre. The possibility of having to give
him up in a year is heartwrenching.

2756 GIRL OF MYSTERY Mons Daveson
An Australian millionaire is mystified by a secretive waif
who dashes in front of his Jaguar. She won't tell him her
address; so he feels compelled to take her home.

2757 AEGEAN ENCHANTMENT Emily Francis
A physiotherapist loves Greece! But her patient's older—
and hopelessly overbearing—brother insists she will never
understand their ways and can't belong. Which only makes
her more determined than ever to fit in.

2758 HUNGER Rowan Kirby
When a Canadian writer and his troubled daughter invade
an English bookshop owner's solitude, can she balance her
hunger for love with her fear of being hurt again?

2759 PAGAN GOLD Margaret Rome
Valley D'Oro's mining magnate accuses a visiting
Englishwoman of squandering her family's fortune to trap a
man of substance. Yet he defends his family tradition of
purchasing brides from impoverished aristocrats!

2760 SKY HIGH Nicola West
An amateur hot-air balloonist refuses to be grounded by an
unfair job interview. She knows exactly where she wants to
be: suspended somewhere between heaven and earth—in
this man's arms.

Available in April wherever paperback books are sold, or
through Harlequin Reader Service.

In the U.S.
P.O. Box 1397
Buffalo, N.Y.
14240-1397

In Canada
P.O. Box 2800, Postal Station A
5170 Yonge Street
Willowdale, Ontario M2N 6J3

WORLDWIDE LIBRARY IS YOUR TICKET TO ROMANCE, ADVENTURE AND EXCITEMENT

Experience it all in these big, bold Bestsellers— Yours exclusively from WORLDWIDE LIBRARY WHILE QUANTITIES LAST

To receive these Bestsellers, complete the order form, detach and send together with your check or money order (include 75¢ postage and handling), payable to WORLDWIDE LIBRARY, to:

In the U.S.
WORLDWIDE LIBRARY
901 Fuhrmann Blvd.
Buffalo, N.Y. 14269

In Canada
WORLDWIDE LIBRARY
P.O. Box 2800, 5170 Yonge Street
Postal Station A, Willowdale, Ontario
M2N 6J3

Quant.	Title	Price
_____	WILD CONCERTO, Anne Mather	$2.95
_____	A VIOLATION, Charlotte Lamb	$3.50
_____	SECRETS, Sheila Holland	$3.50
_____	SWEET MEMORIES, LaVyrle Spencer	$3.50
_____	FLORA, Anne Weale	$3.50
_____	SUMMER'S AWAKENING, Anne Weale	$3.50
_____	FINGER PRINTS, Barbara Delinsky	$3.50
_____	DREAMWEAVER, Felicia Gallant/Rebecca Flanders	$3.50
_____	EYE OF THE STORM, Maura Seger	$3.50
_____	HIDDEN IN THE FLAME, Anne Mather	$3.50
	ECHO OF THUNDER, Maura Seger	$3.95
_____	DREAM OF DARKNESS, Jocelyn Haley	$3.95

	YOUR ORDER TOTAL	$_____
	New York and Arizona residents add appropriate sales tax	$_____
	Postage and Handling	$ .75
	I enclose	$_____

NAME _____

ADDRESS _____ APT.# _____

CITY _____

STATE/PROV. _____ ZIP/POSTAL CODE _____

WW-1-3

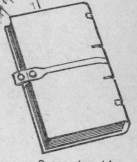